PIMP OF DA RATCHETTS

BOOK 1 OF THE PIMP OF DA RATCHETTS SERIES

BY HITACHI CHOPARAZZI

PIMP OF DA RATCHETTS
BOOK 1 OF THE PIMP OF DA RATCHETTS SERIES
BY HITACHI CHOPARAZZI

Editing and Interior Layout by Urban Book Editor
Cover Design by DJ Designs

Published by Chop-A-Style Publishing, PO Box 693, Chino Hills, CA 91709.

Printed in the United States of America.

ISBN-13: 978-1-7320886-0-3

ISBN-10: 1-7320886-0-8

Library of Congress Control Number: 2019951618

10 9 8 7 6 5 4 3 2

First Edition

This is a work of fiction. Names, characters, businesses, places, events, locales, and incidents are either the product of the author's imagination or used in a fictitious manner. Any resemblance to actual persons, living or dead, or actual events is purely coincidental.

ACKNOWLEDGMENTS

I'd like to give all due praise to Allah! Shout out to my GMa Lawson, all my sisters in the middle of the map, and my REAL family, too. All my lost loved ones may y'all rest in Harmony. Lil Bro Peppy, G-Pa Lawson, Unc Dale, and all my project family Day ones. May Allah bless y'all souls. My kids Kolany Jr., Pierre Kydale, Kylan, and China Doll; Daddy loves y'all indescribably unconditionally. Chop-A-Style Pub—Free Choparazzi, AKA Hitachi Himself!

I want to take the time out to do a special thanks to a very special friend who believed in me and took time out of her busy schedule to type up and edit my manuscripts. I would love for you to be the CEO of Chop-A-Style Publishing.

Thanks, Lady Ty, the world needs more people like you in it. I love and respect your realness because it's rare these days. Some people can't even get their mamas to be real with them. Peace and Blessing to you and those you hold closest.

I got a hundred of these bangers in my head. And I can't stop—won't stop until I get to the top. I got prequels, sequels, trilogies, etc. I love all y'all that love me and my works of twist and events of stories are for your entertainment. The illest-realest! I got my unique style, and I'm going to push it. Chop-A-Style Pub.

Table of Contents

PROLOGUE

5:24 a.m., Baton Rouge, Louisiana, January 2014

"*EEKK—EEKK—EEKK!* Ooo… Ooo… Yesss, FUCK ME! CUM on ME, hurry!" Lela screamed as she faked an orgasm with theatrical moans. She kept twisting her neck back, looking like a straight crackhead that she was.

"Pssh…Hhuuh—SHIT! Fuck, Mama!" Twan said groggily, half-asleep with an aching hangover as he smacked his lips and banged on his wall.

The noise grew more rapid and seemed to echo on Twan's eardrums as the vigorous pace increased, which caused Twan to snap out of his drunken comatose state. He couldn't believe it. He had gone super hard at the club on the Southside, popping red Mac Dre's triple stacks and snorting a few lines of them white Mollies, too.

Twan felt like he had just gotten home. He mustered up all his energy and stumbled to his closet to grab his sawed-off .410 gauge as he squinted from the rays of the Louisiana sunlight.

BOOM! "Ahh!—Ahh! Twan! No—Twan, don't shoot! Don't do it! No, baby!" Mama Lela said as her son kicked the door down and barged in with a shotgun at shoulder height.

Twan caught his Mama taking a full pull off her ratchett homemade crack glass pipe while a white trick was humping her like a bunny rabbit from behind with his pants dropped down to his knees as he stood over the bed.

BAMM—SSWAHTT!

"PPPpphh…pspphuuh! SHIT!" the white man cursed as he spit blood and four of his side teeth because of Twan's thrust of the .410 stock. That's all he remembered before the shotgun came down on the crown of his head and knocked him unconscious with his pale dick still in his hand.

Twan dropped the .410 to his side and rushed his Mama, viciously snatching her up by the roots of her nappy new growth.

"STOP, TWAN! Boy—I'M YA MAMA!" Lela screamed.

"Shut up, you stupid crackhead hoe! What I tell your nasty ratchett ass 'bout turning them broke-dick dirty tricks in here, huh— bitch?" *BAMM!*

"Ouch, Twan! Why, you… Ouch—STOP! Okay, stop!" Lela said. Tears sprouted as her own flesh and blood hit her in the ribs with the gauge.

Twan knew she didn't feel shit. She wasn't begging for mercy, yet. The crack had her whole body numb.

"Bitch—Didn't I tell you if you turning tricks and sucking dicks to get a quick fix, to come spend with me, hoe? I still got a half ounce! You my Mama. I'll give you a double up! But—nawh! Bitch, you want to choose to go spend with them niggas under the bridge. The same ones who killed your eldest son instead of with ya only son left! It's ya fault my lil bruh gone, too! Bitch!" *POWW!* Twan went on a raging rant before he backhanded the shit out of his Mama Lela.

DOOM! Then the .410 went off!

* * *

Neese pulled up on 32nd Street just in time to see her boyfriend getting roughhoused and slammed by the BRPD after being handcuffed. She saw the fire truck and a small, fragile body strapped down on a stretcher. At first, she thought *Twan done gone too far this time and killed his own Mama!* Then, she saw Mama Lela's little frail hand move. Right then and there, she knew that Lela was high and probably was turning a trick in her house, despite how much she and Twan had bumped heads about it before. Twan hated when she did that.

"How much is his bond, Officer? And what's his charge? Domestic violence? That's his Mama. She may say she pressing charges, but don't never ever show up for court!" Neese said, disrespecting the law. Then, directing her convo to Twan as she blew him a kiss, "Twan, fuck these bitch-ass porky pigs! I'll be down there to bond you out, babe!" Neese said, disrespecting the law, and then directing her convo to Twan as she blew him a kiss.

CHAPTER 1: Twan

Twan was fresh out of the Baton Rouge County Jail after doing eight months and found Neese waiting outside in her all-black 2009 Impala on 22-inch chrome Bellas.

She hated when Twan went to jail, especially the lengthy process for him to get released. It was like them crackers slow played and took all day to let her nigga go, but they were fast to book his ass in there.

She reclined low in the seat with her Ray-Bans on listening to "Na Na." As Trey Songz blew the hook, she swayed her neck side to side in a slow rock, provocatively.

Then she shook her head and sucked her teeth as she watched bony-ass Twan with his matted afro trying to pull up his pants. She could see they had taken his belt and his shoelaces too by the way his Reebok Classic's tongues were flopping all over the place as he crossed the street.

BOOM-BOOM! "Come on, bitch, let's bounce! Crank this mufu up, Neese—"

"Oh, hell nawh—boy, don't be bangin' all on my hood! Pssh… see, damn, Twan, you play too much, punching my hood. Now you dented my hood. You ain't gonna pay fo my shit," Neese said as Twan pounded on her hood twice, then slid across the top of it celebrating his freedom.

"Shut up and head to my mama's house," Twan said.

Neese stared at Twan hard with his two ratchett gold fangs that were dull and peeling from not taking care of them and too much alcohol, blunts, and Blacks-N-Milds. *Ugghh!* she thought to herself and second-guessed why she loved him so much.

Twan glanced back at Neese. She was looking extra thick, with her pink, juicy, sexy lips. His dick jumped and ached for her. Her orangish-sandy-brown hair took on a golden hue when the sunlight hit it. She was a bright-skinned Creole and a sexy 5'5" and 135 lbs.

Twan had snatched her up when she first came from Lake Charles, Louisiana. He knew he had to catch her while she was young, dumb, and full of cum. She had been only 15 years old, and he was 17. He had popped her cherry and was all she knew until he started going in and out of jail. Then, she turned into a straight Dora, the curious sexual explorer with hazel eyes.

Twan didn't give a fuck. He was a natural-born pimp. He started macking on girls in the fifth grade, playing them all for their lunch and milk money. By the time he started junior high school, he was smoking weed, tricking girls out their panties, breaking them, and then shaking them. Headache and heartbreak!

Neese was the only one dumb enough to keep coming back even after he repeatedly broke her heart and crushed her feelings low to the earth. She truly loved his dusty ratchett ass. Somehow, she believed him.

Twan loved fucking Neese because anything goes. He loved how they role-played and talked crazy to each other when they both were on a good one.

His mind faded further, rewinding a memory of a threesome they had with one of Neese's homegirls. He loved the sexy, thick chocolate thighs and cupcake soft assed lesbian tooted up in the air as Twan stroked her from the back, watching Neese get her phat wet pussy being licked like a kitty cat licking itself with long, passionate strides of the tongue.

Neese had gotten off with no shame in her game like she did it before and got down with a girl one on one. Twan didn't put it past the sneaky freaky red-yellow bitch. They looked at each other like neither one wasn't—shit! They gave each other direct eye contact. She creamed all over the other bitch's warm, strong slippery tongue, while Twan skeeted all over her back and hair. They pushed the chocolate bone out of their way while they got to it raw. Twan was punishing her that night with his front left stroke game. He had her legs propped behind her ears. He knew how to make the pussy pop out.

"I wanna be with you—I wanna be with you! I wanna be with youuu!" The ringtone played out Future's latest hit single on Neese's Galaxy S4 as it snapped Twan out of his demonic-like trance.

Neese hurriedly touched the screen, acting like she went to answer it as she pressed ignore in one quick slick motion like she'd done it a million times before. She had hoped Twan didn't peep her game. Her toes cringed in suspense as she got paranoid and nervous at the same damn time. She almost felt her face burning in a stinging open-hand slap from Twan with his sandpaper-rough hands. She just braced herself as she peeked at Twan, who was staring at his raggedy Mama's house as she pulled into the driveway.

She hated that look he had. *Uugghh!* she thought again. Neese knew Twan's screw face. She could see he was thinking about which ways he can twist and bend her sexually or how many fingers could he fit up her ass—yuck! She hated every time he or any of her side piece jump-offs got fresh out of jail.

Twan slammed the door of Neese's car. Neese told him to stop slamming her door so damn hard.

"SHUT UP, BITCH—GRAB YA PHONE and bring ya faggot ass on, Neese!" Twan yelled as he snarled his lips, showing his ratchett gold fangs like an angry black wolf and motioned with his left index finger. Neese sucked her teeth and complied. She stormed toward the house, switching her ass like she was Sasha Fierce in her red six-inch heels.

Twan saw how junkie his Mama left the house and went straight to his room, which had been ransacked. That's how he always found it when he first got out of the county. By the age of 20, he was used to ten to 20 crackheads clucking and pawning all his shit. This time he didn't even have a clean pair of boxers left, let alone a pair of his J's. He hated his mama!

Neese followed behind him, looking to see if his mama was there. To nobody's surprise, she wasn't.

"Peeweehh!! Ugghh... Oh—hell nawh! Nope, Twan, we ain't fucking in here! It smells like pickled pig funky feet! I rather give you some ass in the back seat! Now open the windows, and let's go!" Neese shouted, aggressively giving commands as she held back her head and squeezed her nose pinched shut like she had a bloody nose. She was in complete disgust.

Twan told her to lay her punk ass down and roll up a blunt as he slammed and locked his room door, then snatched the purple Crown Royal bag from her and popped half the white Molly, then tossed Neese the bag. He told her to pop a whole Molly and sprinkle his other half on the Kush as he took a hefty swig of Crown Royal.

Twan started throwing some old clothes straight out the open windows in his room. He sprayed Febreze, then even sprayed some on Neese's funky ass too, being funny.

Neese kicked Twan and threw the laced Kush/Molly blunt at his chest. Then she tried to take his head off with her pink Bic lighter catching him in his funny elf-shaped ear.

Twan grabbed his ear, picked up the blunt, and fished out the pink lighter from the sea of dirty clothes.

They smoked the laced blunt and sipped on the Crown Royal till their blood was warming their skin. Twan was zooted and on stuck mode with a silly smirk on his face like he'd landed on the moon.

Neese's tolerance was higher than Twan's at that time. She wasn't fresh out the County Jail. She looked at her dude and realized Twan called himself trying to grow some baby dreads. He didn't know how horrible he looked. It just wasn't him, especially how he called himself a pimp with his ratchett ass. She still felt her thong wet as her legs gaped open. Her hot pussy churned.

She got up and took off her heels and then her black velvet one-piece. She never wore bras. She didn't like or need them to support her 32B cups. Then she peeled her sticky wet pink thong down her thick yellow thighs and flung them at Twan.

Twan's dick was throbbing with anticipation as he watched Neese strip down. She had the sexiest pink perky nipples with pepperoni-size areolas. Twan quickly drew down on her as he freed his hard bulge out of his 501 jeans.

"No—not yet, babe. Let me wash you up first. Let's get that County scent off ya first, then we can play, and you can have it all ya way like. It's ya 21st birthday, babe! You can even fuck me to ya favorite ratchett ass rapper 2Chainz. I got all his new shit on my phone, babe! C'mon," Neese said in the sweetest horny voice ever with a strong Louisiana accent. She would speak Creole slow to Twan during their sexcapades.

She pulled Twan by the hand into the bathroom, turned the hot water on high, and finished undressing him. She stroked Twan's crooked dick, then kissed it, teasing him as she tasted his pre-cum. She loved his hook dick, not only because he could fuck her good, but it was a way for her to know who he was fucking because every girl would run her loose-ass mouth. And Twan was too dumb to catch on. It was funny to Neese because he thought she was just that damn good and just loved to see her fighting hoes out of their clothes, ratchett color weaves, and wigs.

She washed Twan's chest, back, and all between his ass cheeks. She always liked to try to take shit to a whole other level, but Twan wasn't with all that homo shit and put his hand firmly around her neck.

Neese smiled and said sweetly, "All clean. Now we can play."

Twan released her neck and then watched her touch her toes in the shower spreading her luscious apple bottom, showing Twan all her pearly pink insides.

Twan penetrated slowly as he stroked her, catching an eyeful watching his rock-hard dick disappear as he went in and out. Then he had to catch himself as he started pounding her with hard thrusts. He pulled out to calm himself down.

"Let's go to the room," he said.

Neese couldn't believe him. She was rolling super hard and was ready for Twan to do whatever he pleased and had been thinking about doing to her for those eight months he'd been away.

Patt-Patt! "Ooo—Yess, babe, that's how I want you to smack my ass just like that while you hit it from the back… Ohh, ya know I love dat shit, babe," Neese proclaimed. She was folded over with one leg on Twan's bed and the other on the floor.

Twan pushed her down further by the nape of her neck until her chin dug into the mattress, causing her to toot it up harder.

Twan didn't go slow or have no mercy on no hoe, especially Neese's slick, fast ass. It was like a grudge fuck every time he came home because he knew she was out fucking for nothing when she should have been charging all them tender dick vics. All those niggas were big-time tricks and not really about their cash or else they'd mash on all hoes like Pimpin' Twan.

After Twan got his rhythm back and knocked the rust off his stroke, he was vibing with Neese as she began to throw it back at Twan. When she did that, she was about to start getting loose and cumming fast.

Twan began to freak her clit sideways real fast. Then he pat the clit firmly like he was pressing a button on and off.

"Ooowee… Babe—Can I creme all ova ya dick, please? Yesss! Ooo—Twan, I miss this dick, I swear I do! Babbbeee—O!" Neese whimpered in the ecstasy of endorphins that were ten times increased and intense. Her pussy was as open as the ocean and soaked as the sea, and she creamed all over Twan's dick.

Twan felt her pussy contracting, legs shaking, and juices flowing. Right then, he knew he had her open, and it was time to turn up despite how much he missed her sweet Creole wet-wet. This is how he smashed on all his hoes. When you got any hoe loose, you could tell her anything. She would go for anything just to cream over and over. And they would be back time and time again! Trey Songz would that sing sex ain't better than love, but Twan knew it was, and he wasn't going to wake the next man.

Nawh, they were all suckers caught in a trick's web. He wanted to help show the bitches how to vic all the tricks.

Twan went super hard, digging deeper in her, then put one of his feet by Neese's chin on the bed as he got sideways from the back and was going up and down still from the back. Neese had them dreamy sex eyes and made different fuck faces as Twan beat it in and out. She was going berserk, moaning and panting like a bitch in heat.

"Bitch—You luv dis pimp? Huh—hoe?" Twan yelled, bubbly as he remained in control of his position, despite how sweaty his forehead and nose were.

"Yeahh…Twan! Yesss—I do—I swear I love you, babeee. Ooo… Twan, I love you ONLY, babee…" Neese moaned. She tried to sound super nasty, putting two on ten as she felt the beads of sweat off Twan's forehead dropping on her back.

"Well, get ya phone then, bitch! Get it! And call ya mama too!" Twan switched up on her with an aggressive tone.

"No—Twan, babe, I ain't 'bout to call my mama, Boy! Ya trippin'. They know I love and keep going back to this dick!" Neese replied in a severe tone.

Patt-Patt-Patt! "Bitch, what I say, huh??"

"Okay, Twan. Damn it, Twan, ya too crazy, boy! Damn, okay, I got the phone, shit! I'll tell her! Fuck it!" Neese said as she pressed home and then put it on speaker, annoyed. Twan was going too far and was drunk.

Neese threw her phone down and tried to control her muffled moans in the pillow.

"H-Hello?" Patricia answered.

"M-Mom, I-I-I love T-Twan, Oow—" Neese proclaimed as she buried her face back into the pillow helpless. She couldn't help it. She was too geeked up off the pills, and Twan had her too open. She couldn't front or lie. He was doing his damn thang, and dick game was right back up to par. Maybe this was why she loved him? —Nawh, she knew this was why she loved him and was all about his ratchett, no-good ass.

"Unt-unhh no—Hell no, y'all not having sex, Neese? I know you ain't disrespecting ya dear mama like that shit!" *Click!* Neese's Mama said in shock, feeling disrespected, ready to beat Neese and Twan's ass!

"Pssh…see, Twan, you fool! I told ya drunk ass, dummy. Now get off me for that—nigga!" Neese said, trying to squirm away, slouching down so Twan could pull out of her.

"Bitch! Shut up and call her back! I want you to tell her it again. I ain't satisfied yet! Now come here!" *PPatt!* Twan provoked her as he pulled her back up by her thin 21-inch waist and smacked her ass.

Neese loved when Twan snatched her small ass up and didn't give in to her. She immediately picked up the phone and touched the screen again.

"Hello—Neese! Gurrl, if you don't stop playing on my phone—"

"Mom, I—shittt oohh… Damn it, Twan, stop making me moan,

fool! —Mom, I love Twan—" Neese screamed, cutting off her Mom.

"Bitch!" *Click!* Patricia cursed her in Creole and hung up. Then she threw the phone across the room.

Twan told Neese to come here as he pulled out and held his stiff, throbbing dick. Neese was happy, thinking it was about time he was about to cum. And she didn't care if it went all over the place or her face. Because this fool was drunk and rolling hard! Then she began giving him some intimate tongue time as she bopped up and down 'til she gagged and couldn't swallow no more of him.

Twan loved Neese's head game. It had a way of working a spell on you. He knew she was Creole, and they were notorious for that voodoo, black magic, roots shit! Maybe he shouldn't have called her Mama. What if she made his dick fall off?

"Bitch, nope! You ain't done yet! Call dem niggas you been fucking while I was in the County, hoe—"

"Please…Twan, stop playing, boy! What niggas??" Neese intervened in denial.

Patt! "Bitch, andale!" Twan yelled as he slapped his dick out her mouth. Neese held her red stinging cheek as she scrolled through her phone and put it on speaker.

"What's gravy, baby? Where you at right now?" the nigga answered.

SMACK-SMACK SMM-SMMATT!

"Do you hear that, RoRo? Huh? Listen now! —" *SMMSMMAT-SMACK* "Huh? Ya hear dat now? That's them snap, crackle, and pop noises! —"

"Yeah…bitch, I hear you—I know you miss this dick too. I hear you playing with ya sex toy!" RoRo cut Neese off, anxious for some phone sex and some attention just like a bitch and the little hoe he was. He thought for sure he was going to get it popping.

"Nawh—Nigga, that's me slurping my dude's big dick like a l-l-lollipop—"

"Fuck you, rat-bitch!"

"Nawh, fuck you! With ya fat tricking short dick ass! Lose my number, punk!" *Click!* Neese said as she hung up and continued to suck Twan viciously at top high Internet speed! She felt him premature ejaculating lil increments and knew that shit turned Twan on! She didn't give a damn about that nigga. Fuck him and his feelings. She rather it be better a nothing-ass nigga that she has no feelings for than her own mama. Plus, it took Twan's direct attention off her mom. She wasn't going to do that one no more this night!

"Bitch, dat ain't it! Ya ass ain't slick! Keep sucking my dick like you luv me and call that other nigga and tell him you charging him for this ass now. He gotta pay now! Fuck dat. I'm home. Ya pimp, not a simp-hoe!" Twan said fiercely as he started chopping and popping all slick. He popped his nails out after every single word with both hands, never taking his eyes off her. Neese knew to always give him direct eye contact when she gave him head. If not, Twan felt disrespected because he tries to keep it pimping. He would always tell her that's how she should salute a pimp. But all her tricks she did it with her eyes closed and visualized it's Twan.

Neese picked up the phone, trying to peek at the screen as she was moaning with the dick in her mouth like it tasted good and if he was fucking her mouth, just as he trained her to do. He believed Neese thought she could feel it in her pussy every time she sucked his dick, especially after that one time he talked to her so dirty that he made her cum while she was giving him some Becky! Really, he was all in her ear, talking slick and licking the rim of her earlobe.

"What's Gucci, baby?" a nigga answered with a heavy New Orleans accent. "Hello? Neese, why you just didn't text, baby? H-Hello, Neese, you there? What's that popping noise, bitch? What, you on a pill this early? It ain't even dark yet," he said to an awkward familiar noise that finally clicked! "Hold up, bitch. You know what number you called? You had to have ya screen unlocked and hit my shit by accident. But I know you can hear me cuz I hear ya nasty ass slurping and slobbering, trifling-ass hoe!" he said, getting heated.

"Ummh...N.O.? Peep game, nigga! If you want this pussy, ya got to pay for it now! And I need a stack every time. You owe, nigga! My pimp Twan is home, and that's whose dick I'm breathing on right now, okay, sweetie? You know the number. I gotta go 'cause my babe 'bout to cum!"

"Bitch, I'm from the Mighty Nine where they don't mind dying, hoe! 9th Ward, bitch, New Orleans. I'll melt you in and that faggot-ass nigga name Twan. I'll get wet and wet up ya mama's crib, bitch!" *Click!* N.O. stated with his jaw jacked to the side, showing his top row of gold slugs on fire as he clutched his German Uzi.

Neese went to going super hard on Twan's head. She felt his thighs jolt as his whole body jerked. She knew it was time, and that call did the trick with Twan's kinky, twisted, dark fantasy.

Then quickly leaned back, squinting her eyes as she stroked the shaft of his dick up and down swiftly like a three-time all-pro champ.

"Ug-ugg-ugh...Fuck, bitch, yeah—O—Damn, bitch...U-ugh-yeah, bitch!" Twan said as he discharged all 8 months all over her face and hair. Her forehead to chin was soaked, dripping with his little babies. He even skeeted all in her eye orbits. One of her eyes was globbed shut.

Neese felt the warm cum on her face and felt her clit tingle and harden as her pussy contracted and climaxed too. She was a true natural freak and had a natural gift to come easy. Or just more sensual than the average girl. Whatever it was, Twan loved it and used it to control her. He knew it.

She hurried up and picked up her phone and touched the camera to take a selfie as her legs trembled in small waves of climax.

Twan watched Neese squint out of a half-open eye as she took selfies of his cum all over her face. She was flicking her gold tongue ring all around her lips in the cum as it slowly dripped sticky. She must've taken a dozen selfies in seconds like the paparazzi, and then pressed send.

Twan fell back on the bed, trying to catch his breath and slow down his beating chest. He felt his irregular heartbeat and effect of the cocaine in the e-pill. He watched Neese wipe her eyes with her left hand to see her way to the bathroom.

"I wanna be with you! I wanna be with you! I wanna be with youu!" her phone ring back went off. She sucked her teeth and quickly snatched up her phone as her sudden stop made her yellow phat ass jiggle. She knew Twan was watching and pulled both stunts on purpose—to let Twan know that she was that bitch and his bottom hoe for life, no matter what other bitch he thinks could ever be or take her position!

"Hello? What—Nigga, damn?" Neese shouted.

"Bitch, when I see you and that turtle-looking ass nigga, duck, cuz I'mma bust! I put that on the Ninth Ward, bitch! You a walking dead loose bloody pussy, bitch! Sending me pictures of ya face all skeeted on. I'm 'bout to put ya nasty hoe ass on Instagram, and maybe you'd get more dates on ya fish site, hoe!" *Click!* N.O. said viciously. He spit every word as a promise. Neese or Twan couldn't hear the venom in his words. They were too busy caught in their own power cloud and stuck on each other...

Neese came out of Twan's stank-ass bathroom butt naked. Twan watched her gaze at him like he was the Lion King. She wiggled her apple bottom then rolled it from side to side as if she was vibing to some stripper music.

He signaled for her to come on, anxious for round two. Neese shook her head No slowly as she watched Twan grip his dick, excited.

"Nawh, babe! Please, let's go to my granny's house cuz I don't feel like hearing my mama's shit. And nigga, you got me sore and swollen down there. I'll give you some more ass in the morning, Babe. Now, c'mon. Let's go! Please…" Neese said faded, using her soft voice, the same one she used for her tricks and all her clients.

They got dressed and headed to Neese's Granny's house as they drove slowly, sipping on the rest of the Crown Royal.

CHAPTER 2: Neese

Neese told Twan she was Gucci on the Crown Royal as she pushed the bottle out of her face. She was mad at herself for having a girl moment. She had been looking in the rearview mirror from side to side, sucking her teeth viciously.

Why wouldn't the side of her hair grow by her temple?? She was insecure about her patchy bald spots. She would always tell people it was from wearing her ponytails too tight.

She also knew Twan didn't like it because that was always one of the first mean things he would say to her. Then again, he probably only said something to get a reaction. Twan knew it struck a deep match. The pill was wearing on her and taking a negative effect.

Thank God she was at her Granny's house. She hit her alarm as she stormed up the steps. She looked over at Twan, who stood 5'11, 170 lbs. Twan was slim with a thin build, the runt of his family. Twan wasn't light-skinned or dark-skinned. He was a caramel chocolate color, which emphasized his gold fangs.

"Neese? Girl, what in the world do you think you doing now? Following ME? What did you think? Now you gonna bring Twan around me? Let me guess—to have sex in front of me and tell me how good y'all freaky wild sex is? Hell nope! BYE, Twan!" Neese's Mama yelled, red in the face.

Neese snapped out of her emotional rant as her mood changed in a flash, now realizing she walked right past her Mama's Durango.

"Mama, fine, we'll go to the house, but I'm tired and drunk! You know Twan can't drive my car anymore! —"

"Shut up, Neese. I ain't want to drive that raggedy-ass Impala. I got whips put up! Pimp shit, not buckets!" Twan said defensively, interrupting Neese as her Granny looked at all of them like they were a hot mess. She just wanted to feed Twan.

Neese's Mama snatched her keys off the table and slammed the front door, flicking Neese and Twan both off, poking out her bottom lip with an upside-down smile.

For the next few days, Neese didn't see Twan. It took a total of five days before he came to see her at her Mama's house. It had been two weeks now, and Twan only saw her twice and fucked her once. That motherfucker, she thought.

When he did come around, it was to get some money. Twan had her turning tricks at the truck stops and would send her on the Greyhound to Shreveport and Boothville. She loved Shreveport because her Granny used to live there before she got older and moved to Baton Rouge. Neese worked the hot spots. He kept her in short skirts, showing off her yellow Beyoncé thighs, which was sure to catch her a date. It never failed.

Neese even got her right bottom row of teeth set with open-face gold crowns. The trim around her teeth was gold, which looked sexy to all the hood niggas. Hers wasn't as raggedy and cheap as Twan's were. She had gone to the dentist's office and gotten them done right.

She kept texting Twan. He wouldn't text back for hours at a time. The last she'd heard her girl Stacy had said Twan was riding three-deep with some hoes and was still at that ratchett-ass strip club on the Southside.

Her last resort was to trick him. She texted him, telling him she had come up on a stack for him in attempts to vic him. She needed that drunken Beyoncé Jay-Z love and for Twan to beat it all night. Only he knew how to give her the proper affection and attention she required with her wild, freaky ass. She was an alpha female who needed to be conquered and dominated. She didn't want a soft bitch-ass nigga. You had to go hard on her.

She hated all tricks trying to be sweet, nice, slow, and gentle like they in love and married folks. Even though Twan was scrawny and couldn't fight, she still loved him. She would do anything for him even when he would bring bitches around her and claim them was just some hoes he was smashing hard on and getting it out they funky ass cott.

She hoped Twan wasn't running up in them skanky hoes. *Fuck that!* Neese felt her position switching and slipping. She quickly took off her black lace panties and let her long hair drop down over her bald spots as she covered her ears too. She fixed her red low-cut skirt and hit her Impala alarm off. She was off to find and confront Twan.

This time she took a fifth of Jack Daniels with her, making love to the bottle to take away her pain and sorrow. Jack made it all go away. She felt numb. Then the white granddaddy purple smoke made it that much sweeter as she exhaled. She was ready and down to beat a bitch ass. And that was the way she learned how to fight, over Twan's bony ass.

Something about Twan had hoes flocking to him. He wasn't even balling or a pretty-boy Floyd. Maybe it was his little slick mouthpiece after all because he did have them dumb bitches selling their ass and cashing him out. Truthfully, he didn't need her. Neese stomped on the gas pedal, floating the Impala to the Southside.

Twan heard a vortex engine. He looked over his shoulder and saw Neese's black Impala gunning toward him in the parking lot.

Neese was bubbly when she finally found Twan. She saw him in the parking lot with some hoodrats. He had barely gotten out and already had thrown some Lexani 26-inch rims on a Cadillac.

She jumped out as Twan was jumping in his Caddy. She ran up

to the car and saw three bitches. He had a skinny snow bunny and two yellow bitches. Neese automatically went ham!

Neese crinkled her nose. "Uuggh…Twan, you got these ol' musty hood rats. You need to tell ya new bitches they need to take a bath, douche, and wash their ass!" she said, slick with hateful venom.

Twan was looking down at Neese, shaking his head. He thought, *here goes this jealous-ass drunk hoe being out of pocket again.* Neese was becoming more of a headache than the bread was worth. Twan knew just what he had to do in front of his new bitches, so they'd respect this pimp. That was the key to keeping a hoe's mind. Sometimes they needed to fear a pimp. Twan wasn't a straight gorilla pimp, but he knew how to put the fear of God into his hoes.

Neese snatched the door open and pulled the snow bunny out the Caddy by her blonde hair. Then Neese punched her twice in the face with the paw of her fist.

The little snow bunny started kicking and scratching Neese like a stray alley cat. Twan watched them go at it for a brief minute to see what his new girl had in the tank. Twan had to admit she had heart even though the white bitch couldn't fight.

Damn near the whole stripper joint came outside to watch Neese beat circles around the girl with all her pussy showing. Twan knew Neese was drunk and in heat. Neese had already beaten the poor snow bunny out of her white halter top. Neese had to be at least 10 and 0. She was like a vicious scrapping red-nose pit bull. She would shake their asses up and run them off her territory.

Twan hopped out of the Caddy and snatched Neese up as the snow bunny, who looked defeated, held her bruised, leaking face.

POWW! "Bitch, you out of pocket, hoe! You gonna respect this pimpin'!" *POWW!*

"Awwh—ouch, OK…Twan! Daddy, please! I had some money for you! And you around these Southside hood rats and a white girl too. These bitches will set you up or tell on you! We got history, Babe!" Neese said after Twan backhanded her twice and began to choke her.

He saw Neese's eyes bulging out as the blood vessels popped red in them. Neese sighed out her panted breath, and her whole body went limp.

Twan sat her down slowly as he released his grip. This wasn't his first time choking Neese's out-of-pocket ass out.

He strolled to her Impala and peeled her purse back. He took the only $150 to her name, then tossed out her belongings in the street. He took her keys and chucked them across the road in front of the old fish market.

Then Twan snatched her 7-inch Clarion in-dash screen out. *I'm charging this hoe!* he thought, then turned around to address all the players, pimps, hustlers, and hoes in the noisy crowd. He threw the in-dash in the front of the Caddy and told the white bitch, "Hoe, get in da Lac and pull yaself up, bitch!"

Twan turned up his favorite 2Chainz song as the three 15-inch sub-woofers beat down the trunk of the Caddy, sitting up in the air high dunked out.

"Velcro and I'm sticking to it—Hating I been a victim to it!" Twan spit 2Chainz's bars in sync with 2Chainz verse as he skated slowly out the parking lot of the ratchett strip joint. The Caddy wheel well scraped as Twan turned slowly, curb-checking his 6's.

Neese slowly came back into consciousness as the bouncer poured water down her mouth and splashed her face. She was unaware of her surroundings. She was pissed off and groggy. Twan was M.I.A., and she must have been choked out again. She was walking to her car when the police came into the parking lot. She heard some stripper that hated pimps, especially Twan, putting his hands on her say, "He threw ya car keys over there across the street."

Neese sucked her teeth. The BRPD stopped Neese in her tracks and arrested her for disturbing the peace and towed her car too. Neese kept saying she was the victim in all this.

Neese couldn't bond out till the next day after she saw the judge. She was heated. Here she was, now sober at County booking, stuck with all these stank doped-out hoes all in one tank. And she didn't have on no panties to top it off. She had to pee! She guessed she would hold it until the morning because there was no way she was sitting down on that dirty stainless-steel tank toilet. And she wasn't about to squat down in front of all these hoes! Hell no!

That was until she felt her period coming on. She thought it was a concoction of her having to hold it for hours and being hot at Twan for getting her booked.

She started to act a fool and kick and bang on the tank door as her hormones raged. The County Correctional women officers rushed the tank and tackled Neese, thinking she was still drunk. The sergeant, thinking it was a fight, ran to the tank telling the females to break it up and move out of the way.

After the sergeant realized it was just one problematic drunk girl, she ordered her officers to put Neese in the black chair and strap her down.

Neese started swinging on the C.O.s, resisting. They tasered her. Neese's body froze in mid-air before she fell sideways.

They hogtied Neese like a damn criminal, then carried her around the corner into an isolation cell and strapped her into the cold chair.

Neese sat there spitting on the C.O.s until they put a spit bag over her whole head. She sat there, cramped up for hours as her legs fell asleep. She finally said, "Fuck it!" and released her aching, full bladder. She had already felt the trickling blood spotting all out on the chair. She figured it would help wash some of the stink period blood off the chair that was drying up. She was a mess and disgusted, laying in her stink mess. Neese sat wide awake and plotted how she was going to stab Twan to death.

CHAPTER 3: Baton Rouge

Twan's text messages kept going off. It was Neese threatening him. She kept telling him to give her Granny back the $800 she paid to bond her out for Twan's stupidity. Neese had to sit two whole days in jail because her Mama didn't pay her bond. She didn't care and felt some type of way about Neese and Twan. She wanted to teach her daughter a lesson and told her to call Twan. Instead, Neese had called her Granny to post her a loan.

Twan picked up his phone and turned it off. He looked over at his new bitch named Myrtle da Purple riding shotgun. Myrtle was about 5'1, 118 lbs. and dark purple, that blackberry black. She was a petite thang with a lazy eye, which made her look a bit slow. Most of her clients requested head services, probably to see her cockeyed ass giving them head in amazement.

"Myrtle da Purple Hoe! You see how these hoes do a pimp, huh? They jump all on a pimp phone, blowing it up trynna pay me! See, that was my old hoe. My old bottom bitch. Her head got too big for her shoulders, so I had to knock it off and give da bitch a dose of reality!"

"Oowee…Daddy, I want to fuck dat hoe Neese light-skinned ass up! I can't wait to see her. She never fought a North Houston bitch! We box, bitch! No kicking and scratching. We don't do catfights ova this way, baby! And ain't giving no fair ones, hoe! Anything goes, and we do bust them .80s too, bitch!" Myrtle said with a thick North Houston accent.

Twan looked at her ratchett ass with her maroon wig on like she was a Nicki Minaj Barbie. That shit was tacky. She was a runaway from Houston. She left H-Town when she was 19 years old. She was now 21 and had been bouncing from state to state for two years. She got caught for soliciting tricks in Atlanta and Texas. She grabbed the Greyhound to Cali, but Twan snatched the runaway hoe up from the downtown Baton Rouge bus station, which was one of his usual spots he'd stalk for prey.

He liked her hardcore hood ass. She was a gutta down South bitch that knew how to sell her pussy and use it to get what she wanted in the world. She had three different pimps in two short years. Twan made number four. He didn't care if she was a hand-me-down hoe. He'd take her because he believed she had experience, so he would do less babysitting. He loved hoes he had to fix up. They stayed loyal to the soil longer. He called them fix-me-up hoes. He didn't care; he had just got out the BR County Jail too. There wasn't such a thing as too ratchett for him. Ratchett didn't exist in a pimp's world. They were all cash cows. All prey! And Twan prayed more than a Muslim. Pimp or Die!

She started gyrating in the front seat to the 2Chainz beat like a true H-Town freak. She was a sexy chocolate bitch, he had to admit, but Twan never fucked the bucket-head bitch. *BBOOM-BOOM-BOOM!*

"I should get an app called iTrapp! I been getting money, where the fuck you been!??" 2Chainz ripped thru the airwaves as the 15 subs vibrated the seats.

Twan pulled the Caddy into the best Louisiana BBQ joint on the Southside of Baton Rouge. It was where a lot of players and pimps meet and greet and indulge their taste for smoked BBQ in special marinated sauce. The joint even served some top-quality soul food too.

Baton Rouge was hot and humid, sticky as the night swamp. Twan loved to show off his fresh game. Every time he knocked a new bitch, he showed the pimps and fellas. He didn't want anybody to think he was playing pimpin'. He was serious about his pimpin' for real. He may have had some raggedy hoes, but all of them still go and come back successful. He didn't have a problem sending his hoes off, any time of the day or night, and any place.

Twan stepped out, getting his stroll on with his pimp strut like he was Goldie from the Bay area. Myrtle da Purple opened the BBQ joint door for him.

"Pimp on, Young Twan!"

"Chuchh!" a few middle-age pimps shouted as Myrtle da Purple walked in behind him.

Twan nodded in silence with a serious look on his face as he flashed his two deuces like a real PI!

He looked around at all the vet pimps that had well-known names, cars, establishments, and significant land. Some even were world-renowned from right there in Baton Rouge. There were a few international pimps in the city, although not as many as in Atlanta.

Twan wanted to be respected and known all the way to Jamaica. He didn't want to be just another local pimp getting his run. He didn't want any more good runs. He wanted a lifetime run. Digg that!

The vet pimps with their old hoes looked on. They knew Myrtle wasn't from Baton Rouge for two reasons. She was more country, and they never saw her petite ass around there before, not even growing up there. Plus, Myrtle wasn't jumbo thick. She was small, cheerleader-sized, and made for walking. Her tight calf muscles showed she was a bona fide hoe, a straight street day- and nightwalker beating the concrete with pumps on her feet.

She was just too purple black! Most pimps in BR liked their hoes light, bright, next to white, and believed dark hoes bring dark days. They say a duck makes you a pimp, but a snow bunny lets you pimp. It's a hell of a difference and a headache that'll have a pimp grey in the Feds cross country, especially if they can bamm pimpin' Snooki with no evidence.

"Gigolo bloodline—pimpin' hereditary—all black on 28's. Remind me of February!" 2Chainz spit over the BBQ joint Bose system. That's all Twan heard before the bells on the door began to jingle. He was feeling his nipples like he was the shit bitch and pimp of the year.

Screech...BOOM! B-BBdattt! "Get da fuck down 'fore y'all get laid the fuck down. Everybody now! Old ladies and kids and all— Awww...we got some PIs in here too. Awww, how I luv liq'n pimps! Y'all got that hoe money! It's just as good as dope money! Pimpin' out of luck today and stuck like chuck. It was supposed to be big ballers here today Tuesday meeting up with them big New York boys, yo!" the masked goon in jet-black demanded after he let off shots of the short Kel-Tec 9 mm. Three other goons had run into the joint ski-masked up too. They had jumped out a tinted-out, stolen black Crown Vic.

The whole joint quickly got quiet. It wasn't like out in West Baton Rouge, where all the white folks would've caused pandemonium, screaming and whimpering throughout the restaurant. Even the few kids had covered their mouths and shut their eyes. They were young but not dumb. They didn't want to get shot.

The four goons searched the place and stripped everyone and the cash register. They stripped the pimps out their socks,'s where they found big knots besides Twan's.

One of the goons snatched Twan's pimped-out Gator Air Force Ones he just got from SneakerPimp.com. *Damn! That lil nigga was vicious.* Twan bit his lip; he was pissed the fuck off! Then that same goon pulled Twan's thin ass up off the floor just enough to undo his fresh Versace short-sleeve shirt.

Damn-Damn-Damn it, man—fuck! Twan thought as the thugs ransacked the place and stripped him out his pride. These niggas were ruthless grimy from the Southside for sure. Twan figured it was those niggas from the same rowdy BR projects. He hoped it wasn't them other niggas from the other side of the swamp. He hated the niggas across the water. They had merked his big brother.

The goons were in the joint for a total of two minutes before they skirted out in the stolen Crown Vic.

Usually, after shots were fired in a business, the cops would've been there in record flash time, but not in the Southside of Baton Rouge. The police were never there to save you or help you. May God bless and be with you. And Twan knew they killed Jesus, so he could imagine how they would do a pimp. Everyone loves to hate on a pimp.

"Twan, get up, Daddy! Fuck them bitch-ass broke lil niggas, that's why they ain't got shit! They rather rob than send a bitch. Karma is a motherfucka that spins 360 degrees full circle. Them jack boys don't last long in H-Town. They all end up dead or fucked off in the Penn, Daddy!" Myrtle da Purple said. She sounded country as hell.

She snapped Twan out of his trance as he got up shirtless and shoeless. He never let his chin touch his bird chest, but the pimps could tell his pride was broke. He checked his pockets and didn't realize his Caddy keys were gone too. He quickly looked outside.

"Damn! They done peeled a pimp!" Twan yelled. His Caddy on 6's was gone along with the $4,200 and his 15-inch subs speaker box.

He couldn't trust anybody, and damn sure wasn't going to leave it at his Mama's crackhead house. He didn't believe in banks. They were for suckers. He wasn't ever going to give anybody or business none of his hard-earned money to hold. Shit, he could hold his own money without them white folks in his business.

Twan walked outside with Myrtle. The cool Baton Rouge breeze made him feel like he had started from the bottom, and now he was here. He had only been out for a couple of weeks and got stripped of everything. He hit the outside wall of the BBQ joint. Myrtle went over to grab Twan's hand to comfort her pimp. She told him she would go back to work right now, all night and every night until he gets back right and ten times more than before.

Twan appreciated having a bitch that stayed ten toes down, no doubt. The eldest pimp, Flossie, offered Twan a ride and a couple hundred he had out in his car. Twan gladly accepted and thanked him. Pimpin' Flossie pulled out some nice pimp strings out the back for Twan. They dropped down loosely over his thin frame, but Myrtle da Purple loved them! Especially his white brim. *Now that was pimpin',* she thought. She hoped Twan picked up a few tips from the vet pimp.

Pimpin' Flossie and his vet hoe dropped Twan and Myrtle da Purple off at his hotel room on the edge of downtown. Twan saw the hotel room and noticed the door was slightly open. He stepped inside and then instantly knew what happened. His other hoe, Jada, had smashed out. All her belongings were gone. This made the fifth hoe that had run away from Twan's ass. *Maybe my pimpin' ain't too strong. Nawh, them hoes wake up every now and then.* A pimp's nightmare is for a hoe to wake up or choose up, choosing to leave him for another pimp. *Better that another pimp has the hoe than a sucka or simp,* Twan thought.

He took a deep breath and sat on the hotel bed. Myrtle quickly washed up and called a cab to make her rounds. She would walk around downtown for a few hours and see if she could get lucky and catch a few dates at the bars too. Myrtle da Purple had game and could talk a trick out his whole paycheck. She wasn't a thief, just all fast mouthpiece.

Then she would head out to the truck stops and would hop from truck to truck, catching big dates. Sometimes she would be gone all day and night long. Twan wouldn't trip because she always had a fat grip. The money always was damp and smelt like stank ass! He assumed she kept it stuffed in her honey pot. He would tell that hoe to go wash up and smoke a blunt with her until she fell asleep. Twan always had some cold fast food ready; he ordered a lot for himself and didn't worry about feeding the hoe. He would tell her that he just got the food 30 mins ago. She always believed him even though the McDonald's fries were cold and nasty by the time she got them.

Twan sat in the hotel for 72 hours straight without coming out. Still no word on the Caddy, but he knew it was probably at the chop shop or set on fire. He was thinking of his next move and how he could bounce back the fastest.

He knew he was one hoe away from no hoe! He needed more hoes. But first, he probably needed to invest in an ounce of raw and flip that a few times.

The first night Myrtle came back with $650 and $820 the next night. Hoe money was slow now. That 3rd night Myrtle didn't come home; she must have pulled an overnighter too. *She had better come back with a rack!*

Twan copped a bottle of Southern Comfort on the 4th day. He was in a drunken slumber. Neese had been texting him how sorry she was and telling him she heard about the robbery and how they stripped him of everything. Then she begged him for his location. She knew Twan's thin ass was broken, embarrassed, and in hiding. She already knew his Caddy had been jacked too. She rode around all the usual hotels he frequented. She didn't see any of his little ratchett hoes.

Beep-Beep! Beep-Beep! Twan heard a horn being tapped twice. Only pimps hit their horns twice like that, usually for signaling their hoes or for acknowledging another PI in traffic.

Twan's cell started going off. It was his hoe phone used for his hoes only. He looked down. To his surprise, it was Myrtle da Purple. Boy, was he relieved. He thought she had got booked into the BR County Jail for soliciting. He couldn't even afford to bond her out.

Fuck that hoe! It was cheaper to let her go. He could knock another bucket-head runaway bitch. The name of the game was cop and blow.

"Hello," Twan answered sharply. "Bitch, where you been at, hoe? You calling two days too late! Ya out of pocket and in violation, funky bitch—"

"Say, Mane—Say, Mane! Check this out, Pimpin'. This is Omaha T! I got cha bitch. She choosed a true pimp! I caught her reckless eyeballing. Now, the only problem is I don't want your lil amateur cockeyed bitchhh! So, you can buy the hoe back for a $1,500 finder's fee! So, tell me what's it gonna be, lil Pimpin'? I'll let the musty bitch go! We right outside ya room!" the pimp chopped and popped on Myrtle's pre-paid GO phone.

Twan was speechless. He quickly peeled the hotel curtain back with his index finger. He saw a white 500 Benz with Nebraska plates with a half-breed black/Mexican or black/Indian. He had two long silky braided ponytails that dropped down to the middle of his chest with all gold rings on all his fingers and a short white brim.

Myrtle da Purple sat up in the front seat, pitifully looking directly at Twan pitiful, to see if he would pay her bond and set her free so she can finish going to get the rest of his dough. She knew he'd probably beat her ass, but she deserved it, and she knew it.

She had a problem with being out of pocket and going astray. She already ran away from one of her Atlanta pimps. The other was a true ugly gorilla pimp. He would beat her purple and swell up her face every time. He looked like an orangutan with a long perm.

She had a real problem with being monogamous to one pimp. She always had to see what it was like to ride out with a new pimp and see what his P's was like and game tight. She couldn't help herself and knew she had these issues. She just was a washed-up hoe that had too many different pimps in her short run as a hooker.

She waited for Twan to rescue her and him to punish her any

second now. She felt her insides warm, and her thin G-string get soaked. She cracked a crooked smile with slick intentions.

That feeling went away as ten minutes passed, and they sat parked directly in front of Twan's hotel window, waiting for him to come out to get his hoe.

The pimp beeped the horn twice one last time before driving off. As he pushed the Benz out of the lot, he said, "Welcome to Omaha. I'm a sit yo ratchett ass straight down on the deuce until I can sell you to one of the young up-and-coming P's."

Myrtle sat back in the front seat and crossed her arms in disbelief as the Benz glided through traffic. She liked Twan and thought he was coming out of the Tellie to get her. Now, she was on her way to the middle of the map. She sucked her teeth as a tear skated down her cheek from her lazy eye.

"Bitch—STOP CRYING, HOE! You belong to Pimpin' now!" *Poww!* the Nebraska pimp yelled, then backhanded the shit out of Myrtle. He could've sworn her eye went straight for a second.

Twan sat back and popped the other half of the Louis Vuitton red E-pill. If they weren't the red boys, he didn't want them. He didn't even bother to look back out the window or reach in his pocket to pay Myrtle da Purple's fee.

She had him fucked up and disrespected his pimpin'. That out-of-state pimp in the white Benz could have her and the headache that came with the disloyal hoe. Twan knew that the pimp already had peeled her purse back and made her pay a choosing fee, then tried to sell her back to her pimp. Some pimps do that to stunt and get their names out there. He was vicious, but Twan wasn't going, nor did he care. He just wasn't about to come out his pocket for that hoe. That would've been more embarrassing than getting robbed and stripped out his shirt and shoes at the BBQ joint.

That's how some days turned out in BR. It was full of jack boys, gangsters, hustlers, and pimps, but more fiends and tricks than anything. Baton Rouge, LA, had a population of only 227,818 and was known for its whorehouses back in the day when madams ran the whorehouses before all the famous brothels in Reno, NV, even existed.

Pimpin' was indeed one of the oldest trades to mankind, and it wasn't going to stop with Twan. It was the only thing he knew how to do well. Twan intended to have his own brothels and bring it all back to BR.

CHAPTER 4: Mama Lela

"Hello—Twan??" Mama Lela said thru her GO phone.

"G-Geeah! What's Gucci, Mama?" Twan answered curiously.

"BOY, don't be answering the phone like dat! I'm not one of ya lil flunky hoes. Now, come to the spot and bring a lot! Twan, get cha lazy ass out of the bed! Hurry up before my lil friend leaves!" *Click!*

Twan knew why she hung up before he could curse her dope fiend ass out. He warned her about talking all reckless on the phone plenty of times. *The things crackheads do when they jonesin'!*

He quickly jumped up and put on his Reebok Classics and checked his dope sack of rocks. He had a little over an eightball left. He jumped in the rental and headed to his Mama's spot.

Twan had been selling dope for four whole days now. He didn't ever want to resort to going back to slanging Ya-Yo like E40 says. Every time he hit rock bottom, he needed his Mama Lela to help him get back on his feet.

Neese had saved some money for Twan, but Twan didn't want it or to see her because she just wanted some dick and to throw it in his face. She didn't like to turn tricks but had for Twan before. She just had a brain. He'd go snatch his bread up from that bitch once he was shining back on top again.

"Look at you—Now look at us?? All my niggahs look rich as fuck!" 2Chainz sang the hook as Twan smashed thru the Southside with money on his mind and plotting on his next hoe. He was looking for a victim through the clear windows of the Chevy Lumina rental.

43

Bitches loved it when a pimp did the stanky leg, and that's what he felt like shake-shaking on them hoes and choppin' and poppin' at a hoe, then sit her right down on BR downtown stroll. It was just a matter of time.

However, hoes were not out this early. Mama Lela had him on some early morning crackhead time. Even though he still felt like a million ones, he was on a mission.

He pulled up to his Mama's crib and noticed a silver Kia Sport 4-door car. *Damn it, Jill!* Twan thought to himself as he shook his head from right to left, then puffed the Kush one more last time before putting it halfway out.

He hadn't seen his annoying cousin named Jill in about nine months now. She usually stopped by to see her family in South BR. She was Twan's first cousin. Her Mama was Lela's older sister that was strung out on heroin tough. She had robbed and stabbed a biker to death. They gave her a natural life sentence. The State of Louisiana didn't tolerate a drug-addicted black woman killing a white man back in '97 or ever. Twan hadn't seen his Aunt Leeanne since he was a little boy.

His cousin Jill was half-white and stayed with her old white grandparents in West BR. She was a trick baby, but her father died of throat cancer three years ago. She was a rebellious kid.

Twan knew it was the black in her. She had her ratchett Mama blood in her veins, even though she had been raised around all white people, including her overprotective old daddy.

She used to always sneak over South to go out with Twan to his spots and ride around in traffic with Twan's bad ass. Twan grew out of that shit, plus he knew her half-breed ass would tell if something went down. She just wasn't built for the hood and had no hood sense.

Twan pulled his dope sack from out of his nuts, then tucked it as he walked into his Mama Lela's crib.

"Boy—what took you so damn long? Twan, you play too much. Hurry up, son. We gotta go. He need a 50, and I want a 50 for twenty. I'm ya Mama, Twan. Now c'mon and double me up, son!" Mama Lela greeted Twan rudely.

"Oh yeah, and ya crazy Cousin Jill is here too. Watch out for her, Twan. She growing up too fast and green as a thumb! —Poor child," Mama Lela ranted on. Twan didn't pay her any mind and knew it was just a withdrawal babble until she hit that pipe again.

"Thank you, baby—mmwahh!" Mama Lela snatched the trick by the hand as she kissed Twan and rushed out the front door.

"Hi, Twan! And bye to you, too, Auntie Lela! I miss ya crazy ass, too! Twan, ya mama is smoked out still with a big ole booty. Ha-ha-ha. She's a trip with her ratchett ass! So, what's been going on with you lately, Twan?" Jill said with a preppy, uptown Southern accent.

Twan's mouth was jacked open. He sat there frozen. His cousin was only one year younger than him but had the body of a 26-to-30-year-old woman.

She stood about 5'10", 142 lbs., small waist, some 36 double D's, and a Serena Williams ass. She had a dunk! She was built like an Amazon. Twan couldn't believe it. She was all woman, and all grown up! She had her Mama's genes and her black side showing except for her butterscotch skin and long wavy hair, which hung down to the middle of her back.

She came up and gave her cousin Twan a big hug, squeezing him extra hard. Then Jill told Twan she would smoke a blunt with him and went to the back room.

"Damn, cousin, you grew faster than my lil boney ass. Niggas be trying to test a pimp nowadays in BR! Too many gangstas!" Twan said, insecure. Then Twan noticed how clean the house was. Usually, Mama Lela's shit was junky as hell. It even smelt better; it had a feminine smell like peaches and roses.

Jill came back into the front room and handed Twan some fruit-smelling indo in a glass jar. It had to be at least an eighth with orange hairs and purple buds.

She told Twan to twist two blunts and to look in his dresser for the Cognac blunt wraps while she took a quick morning shower.

As she shut the bathroom door, Twan walked back to his room, puzzled. When he walked in, all he saw was thongs, red lace panties, red-bottom heels, skirts, and a bunch of make-up everywhere. Then he noticed her Louis Vuitton luggage bags all over the place. Suddenly, it hit him. The bitch ran away!

BOOM-BOOM! "Jill, you must've heard I was back in jail, huh? So, you ran away from ya grandparents' home? Ya Daddy gone be rolling over like a Louisiana swamp gator if he knew you was living on the Southside, gurrl! Then ya poor white racist grandparents gonna be worried sick about ya ass. Ya gonna send them straight to they grave. And how you gonna get money, Jill? 'Cause they cutting ya ass off! Don't tell me you dropped out of college, too?" Twan said on the other side of the door, shaking his head.

"Whatever, Twan. I don't care! Aunt Lela say I can stay here in your room because you're always out running them South BR streets with them raggedy hoes—BYE, Twan, let me wash up—and twist the blunt wraps up…please!" Jill said, annoyed, with the shower running over her face.

Twan shook his head at his crazy cousin's hot ass. What a dummy. He put in his 2Chainz mixed CD as he twisted the Humboldt County sticky up.

Jill cut the hot, steaming shower water off just as Twan was sparking his black Bic. She stepped out the shower, patted her curly, wavy hair, then did a half-ass dry-off.

Twan heard the bathroom door creak as Jill stepped out in a white body towel wrapped around her with her hair wet. Twan saw her erect nipples as she sat down on the couch directly across from him. Twan passed her the blunt. She sat there and switched her crossed legs twice like she was red-hot in the ass.

Then she put her bare foot on the glass coffee table and started shaking her whole leg like an excited dog in heat.

"Not-unhh… C'mon now, Jill. Shut ya legs. We family, not friends! I don't want to see ya coochie!" Twan said as he took a glance at her freshly shaved pussy before turning his head like she was blinding him. Scaring him was more like it, though.

"Oops… My bad, cousin. You know I'm a country swamp girl! I've been a tomboy since I was a young girl climbing trees with you, Twan!" Jill replied with a hint of play in her soft voice as she put her feet down and slowly crossed her legs.

They sat there and smoked blunt after blunt until Twan's lightweight ass got stuck. The Kush had him blown. They started off reminiscing, then Jill kept running her mouth.

Twan felt like he knew her whole life story over a blunt. She had told him how she would sneak down from LSU to go to Bourbon St., the Mardi Gras, and Bayou Classic. She loved New Orleans and the French Quarter.

Mainly because her people were French and she had been raised to believe that white is right and black is wrong, she was brainwashed and always had white boyfriends. She always knew it was a part of her missing and knew she was different. Despite how they belittled her and always kept her down, she wanted to be more in touch with her roots. She stopped writing her Mama Leeanne when Twan's Grandma died. Her dad would never let her keep contact with her own Mama. She hated him for that and loved her black Mama even though she was in jail.

Hell, yeah, she wanted to go against the grain and curious about a black man and her heritage, too. It was something that attracted her to a brother. They excel in everything they do, from sports to music to business.

She tried to holler at a few different brothers at LSU, but they all were too preppy and wanted a skinny white bitch. One time at a frat party, she kissed a light-skinned brother, but he ended up hooking and leaving with a chocolate sister. She was lost and didn't get it.

She stopped talking and asked Twan was he listening? Twan didn't reply. He was stuck in a dumb trance-like he smoked some wet Sherm-Moore Stix. She told Twan bye and snugged her towel fit under her arms as she got up and wiggled her body into the cloth tightly.

Jill took a few steps, then Twan heard her towel drop slowly on the floor. He quickly snapped out of it and saw Jill butt naked with a big luscious round yellow booty. God!

She stood there, frozen for a second. Now, she had Twan's attention. She bent straight over slowly, then acted like she couldn't pick the towel up on the first try.

Twan's instincts kicked in. He looked at her fist-size pretty peach. She busted it open one time for him. Fuck it, why not sneak a peek?? Twan was fascinated. She had a pretty pink pussy the size of a glove. He could see through her crevices and her inflated inner pink pussy lips. One was distinctively bigger than the other, but they both flapped out a quarter of an inch. Twan called those outies, which was rare because a lot of his hoes had cute innies. It barely stuck out the crevices. You had to spread their outer lips to see them by the extra loose skin that kept the pussy warm and tucking in.

Jill picked up the towel, rewrapped it snugly, and rushed to the room as she switched hard. Twan saw her juicy firm booty sway viciously from side to side. It bounced from cheek to cheek like she was twerking something.

"Ooo…shittt! —"

"Shut up, bitchhh! Come here and listen up, hoe! You been annoying me my whole childhood and now I see why. I was blinded but see now that I'm on my P's that you been having a big ol crush on me. And you ain't been around no black folks but us! You ain't see no swagged-out fly white guys or nigga until you saw me—bitch! I see what this is about and got you all figured out!" Twan said in Jill's ear in a low tone after he ran up from behind her and snatched her up by her hair. He twirled two fists full of hair as he yanked on her roots, digging his knuckles hard into her tender scalp.

"Un-uhh...Twan! Stop—Stop it," Jill said softly without sincerity.

Poww! "Bitch, shut up, hoe! From now on, we distant cousins. Matter of fact, bitch, call me Daddy! You wanna act like a hoe. I'm a treat you like one!" Twan said sternly as he slapped Jill semi-hard.

She felt the sting on her cheek as Twan flipped her around with her chin against the wall. She couldn't believe how firm Twan's grip was. His skinny ass had power.

Twan kissed her neck slowly as she let out slight moans, which made Twan's dick stand up and salute BR.

Jill felt the bulge in Twan's 501's rising against the back of her ass, then gapped her legs apart and reached back to free his manhood. She just had to feel and see a big black dick. She never had in real life. Internet porn was the closest she'd gotten to one. One time her friend Amber had a dick pic of an 18-incher, down to his knees. The photo had been floating around LSU's campus and was believed to be of an LSU basketball player.

She freed Twan and felt his veiny curved penis. She put it between her legs and massaged her horny, throbbing, swollen pussy. Twan felt the wetness, and the head of his dick swelled to capacity.

"Ooo-O-O-O-Ooo...TWANNN!" Jill screamed as Twan began stroking slowly with full thrusts. Then he started kissing all on her back and shoulder blades as he was still pulling the shit out of her hair and now red scalp.

He reached around and began to rub her clit in small, fast circles with a nice firm press. As her moans became louder, the white started to come out in her. She screamed, "Oh-O-Yesss! Oh, Fuck Yeahhh!"

Twan jacked one of her legs up on the bed and began to take longer strides and picked up his pace as his strokes became hard rhythmic thrusts as he beat it up and went hard in the paint on her ass.

"You my first cousin. Now, you my first hoe—bitch!" *SMACK-SMACK!* "You gonna go empty out ya Dad's and grandparents' accounts, bitchhh! You hear me, hoe?" Twan told her as he smacked both of her yellow ass cheeks ruby red!

"O-Ooo…Y-Yesss, Twan, I-I will, I promise–K–! Yesss–OOoo… just please don't stop. Keep giving it to me, T-Twan—I mean, Daddy!" Jill moaned out the response, letting Twan know she was with the biz and all his. She would do anything for him.

He immediately stopped and pulled out. She turned around and sucked her teeth, thinking Twan just punked out and was through fucking her and feeling guilty. She had no remorse. She loved Twan passionately now. It was too late. He should have never laid dick in her. She would do anything for a dose of that Magic Stix.

Twan already saw he had her dick dizzy, and she had a good tight gushy pussy. It felt like Jell-O. Twan had to stop before he skeeted in his cousin reckless and raw. He knew she was clean or, well, he hoped the bitch didn't have anything. Oh well!

"Bitch, grab that dick! It's all yours now—I don't fuck with Neese no mo! Fuck dat bitch; she's dumb. You got brains and smarts," Twan filled her head up.

She dropped down to her knees happily and got a one-on-one exclusive with Twan's dick. She saw him leaking pre-cum and his famous hook dick. She licked the pre-cum up slowly so Twan could see her skills and watch her put on a show. What Twan didn't know, she sucked dick like a straight-up white girl!

She bopped him up and down slowly and swallowed all of him every time naturally without any gag reflex. She was a pro and knew tricks. Then she took the dick out her mouth, kissed it passionately while looking directly square in his eyes, and began stroking his shaft at a fast pace as she swatted it all on her face and bounced it off her lips.

Twan watched as she proceeded on sucking him up and playing with his balls in her left hand. She was massaging them at the same damn time. He loved seeing her bottom juicy pink lip drag back as she sucked and pulled on it tight and hard as it went up and down on his head.

"Come here, bitch. We ain't done! It's time to make ya thick Amazon ass cum!" Twan said as he pulled his dick out her mouth and threw her on the bed doggy style.

He smacked her ass. It was soft as a marshmallow. It made a cupping noise as he hit it fast and hard off the bed, causing her ass to clap with wave after wave on the big yellow rows of ass.

Then he put his thumb in the crack of her ass after he slobbered down on it like a drooling dog. He worked his thumb in her brown hole as he massaged it first. She never had anal sex or anything up her ass. The white boys were always too scared of that back door because most of them were all shorter than a midget on her knees or minute men without no passion or rhythm.

She was vibing with Twan and trying to throw all that big yellow soft ass back up on Twan while she screamed and shook. Twan pressed his thumb down and felt the thin wall between her pussy and asshole. He felt his dick going in and out her pussy, then pressed down real hard like he was getting thumb printed again at the BR County Jail!

"Oooooo—Shittt Yesss! O-O-O–Daddy! I'm cumming!" Jill

screamed as she squirted fast cum all over Twan and the sheets! Her whole body shook in convulsion as she dove on her stomach from her knees buckling. She didn't know she could ever cum like that or squirt. She believed every woman was promised one good "O" in her lifetime, but she had a feeling Twan could do this to her all the time and conquer her body, just like he probably did with the rest of his hoes. She had wondered why they paid him. Now she knew. The sex was phenomenal and priceless!

"Oh, hell nawh, it's not over yet at all. Sit back up, hoe!" Twan said as he started working her contracted twat. He felt her squirt all over his nuts, and her pussy still pulsing vigorously. She looked back at Twan, stunned with dreamy beady sex eyes as he began to beat it up. Her moans picked up again. She didn't even get a chance to sit in her juices and enjoy the feeling of sexual satisfaction for a moment.

"Bitch, where ya sex toy at, hoe, huh? —"

"It's on the top shelf, Twan—I mean, Daddy. Yasss, grab it please and put it directly on high on my clit, Daddy…O-O-Pleaseee…" she answered, cutting off Twan.

He snatched the little vibrator that looked like a hand massager that she used for a vibrator and pure clit stimulation because it had grids sticking out of it, with her dirty little self. She was going berserk as Twan made her cum back to back. She could barely catch her breath.

"Say Fuck ya dead cracker-ass Daddy, hoe! Who ya Daddy now, bitch! Huh—who loves ya dirty down-low closet freak ass, huh? Who gonna look after you like Pimpin', huh, hoe?" Twan started feeling his nipples again as he went on one of his rants, the same way as he vic'd all his hoes!

"O-O, Fuck my cracker dead-ass, racist Dad! O-O-O…I love you, Twan! I swear you're my number one and only Daddy—I swear it, O-O-O…Yesss, now cum, Daddy!" she moaned provocatively.

BOOM! "Twan, what the fuck—Boy! Oh, hell no! That's why you ain't been answering ya damn phone, boy, and missing money!? Hell nawh, y'all cousins! First cousins. Y'all stop and break that shit up! Twan, I didn't raise you like that, boy! And Jill, I'm telling ya Mama Leeanne on your fast ass. You can't stay here no more. Pack ya shit and take ya disrespectful ass home! Now Twan, get the fuck up! Boy, get ya lil dick out your cousin. She not one of ya hoes. She's blood!" Mama Lela said shamefully in tears after she busted in the door and caught them.

"Twan—okay, stop! That's enough. O-O-O…O-kkay-T-Twan. Please, your Mama's right there. C'mon, we done—OOOooo—" Jill said, trying not to moan, but Twan was showing out and acting a donkey in her pussy. She tried to hold back as she felt herself squirming and cumming fast! She buried her embarrassed face in her bunched-up lace panties and thongs on the edge of the bed.

"Awwhh—Hell nawh, boy!" Mama Lela screamed as she rushed her son. *Bang-Pow-Pow!*

"Shit!" Twan spit as Lela punched him with a cold two-piece and a slap. The knuckle punches landed on his shoulder and directly square on his ear! He turned around, mean-mugging his Mama as he started punishing Jill harder with anger.

Mama Lela squared up her dukes like a dude and then rushed in doing the windmill with her eyes closed and screaming like a wild woman. The white man trick peeked inside the room and knew it was some strange, weird shit going on that wasn't right and saw a fight, too. The hell with the dope. It was time to flee and get the hell out of there.

Twan weaved out of the way, cocked back, and caught his Mama Lela with a clean open hand, dropping her fragile ass to the ground. She quickly jumped up, holding her mouth as she backed out the room, crying.

"Look, Mama. Check this out! You a hoe! Ya older sista is a hoe!

Now Jill is a straight hoe, too, and you know it and see it! She grown and ready for the real world and to spread her little wings! Mama, if I don't manage and pimp on her, then other P's will and use and abuse her. Not so with me, 'cause she family. We all in the same business. I'm a make sure she don't get turnt on to no dope or heroin like her Mama and favorite Auntie Lela! Shit, Mama, you surprised she turnt out like y'all? Only thing I'm a turn her out to is some motherfuckin' pimpin'! Respect it or check it. She stays here and my hoe! Now grab the rest of the dope out of my small side pocket and go get high, you crack-fiend. BYE!" Twan said, telling his Mama Lela straight up how he felt and how it was going to be for now and for sure as he paused in the pussy.

Lela still held her face as she threw 40 of the white trick's dollars on the floor and fished through Twan's 501's, retrieving the dope.

"Ugghh…Y'all nasty, trifling, disrespectful motherfuckers! That's what's the matter with y'all younger fucked-up generation now! Y'all all gay or marrying y'all sibling that Whitney Houston disrespecting daughter shit! She raised her better, just like we did y'all!" Mama Lela talked shit as she gave them an evil piercing stare.

"Please, Mama. Don't act like you didn't notice her now lady curves and her being hot in the ass. That's why you sat her down in my room and ya house. Talkin' about take care and look out fo ya cousin! That's the only way I know how, Mama! So, you didn't indirectly sic me on her? Go somewhere and turn a trick and bring me back some more crack money!" Twan yelled back at his Mama Lela as she paused, cringed at all his sharp words.

Lela threw her favorite framed picture of lil Jill out of the front window, breaking it. She slammed the front door as glass fell everywhere.

Twan pulled Jill's hair and told her to throw her ass back again. He finished gangbanging her pussy as he put his pound game down. She couldn't take it anymore and squirted until she pissed on herself.

Twan pulled out and put his dick directly in her mouth as she deep throated it. All he felt was his head diving down her tonsils relentlessly, which caused him to erupt!

She felt Twan explode his warm discharge down her throat. Twan watched her eat his cum like it was yummy. Then she blew a couple of cum bubbles till they popped, then sucked it all back in and down her throat. Freaky! She loved putting on a freak show, and Twan saw he told his Mama Lela right. She was a straight natural-born hoe. Cousin or not, welcome to the stable—Bitch!

He put on August Alsina's banger "I Luv It!" but Twan put his own Pimp remix to it. "And I'm a keep on pimpin' 'cause I love this shit! And you gonna keep on tricking 'cause you love that bitch…and I luv it!" Twan sang.

CHAPTER 5: Miley

Twan looked down at his screen and watched Neese go ham on Instagram. She was dressed like a bona fide hoe wearing red fishnets looking like a wannabe Beyoncé. He shook his head. Neese had been acting up on Twitter and trying to bash him in front of the whole world ever since she saw him with his nasty-ass cousin Jill. She always knew her half-breed ass had a crush on Twan's trifling ass. They were on some inbreed time, she guessed, but she would be damned if he was going to embarrass her around BR like that.

She saw Twan in the passenger side of Jill's car and tried to run them off the road twice in one day. Twan looked bubbly with a pink brim and red feather tilted in it.

Twan was on the I-79 going northbound to Augustina, LA. Jill had been in touch with one of her college BFFs, some skinny redhead snow bunny. Twan had seen her on Instagram with Jill at one of those LSU frat parties acting stupid and taking shots.

Jill told Twan that Shelly wanted to come down to BR to kick it with her for the weekend. Twan already knew he was going to try to turn the young bitch straight out. Shit, he even thought about setting her down with Jill on the track and putting her on fish, too.

They made it to Augustina at six-ish. Jill pulled over at the BP, where she waited for Shelly.

As Jill walked into the BP, Twan went to take a piss.

"Eewweehh…that nasty motherfucker is pissing outside! Just whip his dick out in public. How ratchett is that?! Look, Shelly! And where is ya BFF at?" Shelly's younger sister said, shocked in disgust. Shelly took a long glance at Twan's wiggly black python as they pulled in front of the BP gas station. Shelly spotted her BFF in a white tennis skirt and a see-through halter top, with clear, 6-inch stilettos. *She's dressed differently…and skanky*, Shelly thought.

"Twerk sumthang—bitchhh! Twerk sumthang—bitchhh!!... Now twerk-twerk, bitch—Now twerk-twerk, bitch!" Chop-Chop's latest strip club hit blared out the canary-yellow Honda Accord.

Twan looked over the roof of Jill's whip and saw a skinny snow bunny twerking her boney ass off! Just like Miley! The only thing was she didn't have an ass at all, so when she twerked, her whole butt bone popped out. She was all backbone with small waves.

Twan just shook his head and cracked a slight smile. Then he saw Jill come out, and the redhead run and hug her tightly, just like an overexcited white girl. She was naturally high off life—no drugs.

Jill helped Shelly drag her LSU gym bag to her car while Twan pumped the gas.

"Daddy—Excuse me, Twan, this is my BFF Shelly! Shelly, this is my cousin Twan from BR!" Jill introduced them.

"Hey-Hi!" Shelly said, goofily as she thought, *Oh no, not the black guy pissing on the tire.*

Twan just gave her a nod in acknowledgment, then frowned as he looked away, just like Katt Williams off *Friday After Next* telling his hoe to dismiss.

Shelly got into the backseat behind Jill's side. She pulled out an e-cigarette. Twan smelt some mango/pineapple fruity smell and looked back to see a shiny flute-like instrument with a blue button that lit up. *What the hell?* he thought. The snow bunny had issues. They don't smoke them fake e-cigs in BR, a new pimp, Kool, or a Black-N-Mild; that's about it!

"She gonna shake it—like a red nose—Shake it like a red nose—I love it when she shake it like a red nose!" Sage da Gemini spit through the Bose speakers.

Twan looked over his shoulders and saw Shelly gyrating and grinding on the backseat! *Damn, she a freaky redhead bitch!* he thought to himself. Jill heard Twan mumbling and glanced at him, looking across at her BFF. So, she quickly looked in the rearview mirror.

"Oh, hell nawh, hoe, I know UR not grinding and twerking on my seats? Somebody needs to get laid, LOL! Why you so turnt up? Are you off them perks? Not again? Twan, don't mind her!" Jill said, embarrassed at her BFF getting so loose.

Shelly just kept going, but Twan knew that hoe was showing off because she was around him and trying her best to act black. He knew this, and she had seen his dick already. She wasn't ghetto by far. Her peeps were probably as rich as a bitch. He admitted she could twerk something pretty good; she just didn't have anything to twerk.

Then it hit him. He would call the bitch Miley! Twan was known for naming hoes, no doubt.

"That's it—MILEY! Fa now on, ya new name is Miley, not Shelly! We don't go by our Gov's down in BR, especially in my line of biz. I'm a pimp!" Twan stated in a stern tone.

She smiled and took a second to reply.

"O-kay, but where did the Miley come from, though? I'm just curious, Mr. Pimp?" Shelly replied, slick.

"Oh, I see ya got a slick ass sharp tongue too, bitch! I ask you the questions, and you answer. It's that simple. Pimps don't answer no question or explain theyself—hoes do! Fake-ass Miley Cyrus trying to twerk with ya flat-ass toosh!" Twan snapped.

She sucked her teeth and looked at Twan as her mouth dropped in disbelief. Nobody had ever called her a bitch to her face before like that. He was serious and had a straight face. And Jill just looked on, driving down the I79 like she was deaf. Shelly's feelings were shot down. She didn't twerk anymore during the entire ride back to BR.

Twan felt good to be back in BR with some fresh game. He loved new merch like new money because that's what new merch always meant. Now it was time to turn the little redhead Miley bitch out. Thank God for drugs and alcohol! He was about to get her off some pills and Grey Goose to get the hoe loose.

They arrived at Twan's Mama's house. He had to get icy first and step out in some Louis Vuitton. After her Dad passed away, she had received money from the accident settlement. He had Jill clear off all her credit cards, and her checking and savings account that her white grandparents saved up for her.

Twan spent ten racz on an icy, fruity bracelet. It was pink diamonds, blue diamonds, yellow diamonds, and a tangerine-colored diamond. Then he had spent 38 racz on two matching icy pinky rings, two flat clear boys that when the light hit it, you could see the rainbows bling and blind you. You couldn't tell Twan anything with his slim frame. He looked at his fresh tapper in the mirror as he slipped on his Louis Vuitton loafers.

Jill quickly snapped a pic of Twan, then struck a pose, squatting down sideways, showing off all her assets and silky hair. Then she took a selfie with him and posted it straight on her Instagram, flexing on them hoes and for all the world to see, not just BR.

Neese saw Twan's Instagram pic with Jill, with her nasty, trifling inbred ass. Neese saw they were going out to East BR's newest hot spot. She wore her red silk skirt with the split on the sides. She had slicked her bald side patches down with dookey-brown gel. She stood in the full-length mirror and second-guessed herself. She could see her thong line and didn't like how her skirt fit, so she slid her tiny lace thong off.

"Wheew—Now that's better! Feels better and looks better too!" Neese said out loud to herself in the mirror as she looked at her round ass cheeks hanging out the skirt half-moon. She instantly knew she was about to turn da club upside down, with bitches hating and niggas gawking and eye-fucking her yellow cakes. Most of all, she wanted Twan's attention. She was sure about to make his skinny ratchett ass miss her so bad that he could taste her pussy on his lips. She had on her Beyoncé "freak 'em" dress. She knew how to make Twan jealous. He would lose his mind when he saw her in the club with no panties, just all thick yellow thighs, and a soft shaved fat pussy!

"C'mon, Miley! I want you to jump into the most scandalous skimpiest shit ya could find. Just try to top ya protégé Miley Cyrus off fa da night. Ya just gotta trust me—'cause all my hoes play they part!" Twan said with a Southside hood accent.

Miley frowned at him and squinted her face like she was straining to see him. She didn't want to agree, but she nodded her head to let him know she understood him. She didn't understand, quite frankly. She had never been around too many black folks. She wanted to kick it and understand Twan. Besides, she loved clubbing. She scrambled to find a skimpy enough outfit to blow Miley out the water. Then she thought *maybe Twan is trying to show me off like I am Miley Cyrus. Who knows?* So, she decided to cut something out of her outfit.

Twan rolled his favorite white O.G. Purple Kush and laced it with a red MacDre thizz pill.

"S-Stop haten—Lil Tunechi got dat fire, and these hoes love me like Satan…Long as these bitches love ME!" Lil Weezy sang through Twan's G-4 phone.

Miley came out in some red fishnet body stocking and a red G-string with a light-tan color fluffy fur over her shoulders draping over her tiny bare titties with no bra or shirt.

"DAMNNN it, bitch, you hoe material all day! I bet we make a million 'cause you a million-dollar hoe, you mothafuckin' snow bunny, Miley!" Twan said with a different high tone of amusement. His eyes lit up like the Southside on New Year's Eve!

"Let's go, hoes! It's tricking seasons. Remember, they gotta pay stacks to play!" Twan said, ready to promote these hoes. He threw on his cranberry LV shades as he snatched the keys to his 2014 CTS rental. He was driving this time, so he could pull up flossing. He floored the Vortec CTS engine as he swayed his head to 2Chainz's "I'm Different!"

Twan pulled up to the packed front street of the new club. All he saw was slick tricked-out whips and dunks sitting high like skyscrapers. Tons of people walked the street, and some were in parking lot pimpin', choppin', and poppin'. He saw all the Southside deep in the crowds. There were even the ratchett hood rats from the projects trying to hit a liq and get chosen. He just shook his head and pulled up to snatch a V.I.P. valet parking.

Twan jumped out with both hoes on his arms as they all walked in sync as one little trio. Heads were turning; there was a lot of hating and jealous teeth-sucking. One bitch even yelled, "Yuck, trashy lil skinny white bitch!" at Miley. Miley didn't even turn her head around in neither direction. She just smiled, feeling all eyes on her and the high tension of the crowd, which made her cling to Twan closer. He felt it and held her firmly, letting her know she was his bitch, and he had her back. They could talk shit and hate on her white ass all they want, but he bet none of them hoes brave enough to step up or try to pull some funny faggot shit.

Twan made his way to the front door and dropped two big faces to the bouncers, which got him right past the long line. Twan got the V.I.P. table and ordered two bottles of rosé. It was on for real. He nodded his head at a few other P's he saw at different tables with their stables. Miley got up and started twerking to the Hannah Montana song. Twan looked at her. It was time to smash on this bitch soon as she and Jill finished their bottle of rosé. He felt the Ecstasy pill as he began to roll hard, sipping on the rosé, scanning the packed room through his cranberry Louis V's for potential hoes to add to his soon-to-be two-hoe stable. Twenty toes weren't good enough. He needed to pimp hard and shine even harder. All he saw was a bunch of hoochies and sack chasers so far, but the big ballers were looking at his fresh merch as well. They were ready to trick and throw bands at his hoes' feet. They wanted to run through a little petite model-size white girl and Jill's Texas thick half-breed ass.

The club was jumping and now jam-packed to the capacity. Twan saw Miley sit her bubbly ass down. She stopped all that twerking. She and Jill couldn't even finish a whole bottle of rosé. They slowed their row. In about 20 minutes, the rosé took its toll on the hoes. So Twan struck out. He slid right next to a slouched-down Miley and got right in her Bluetooth.

"Say, bitch, you belong to me! Ya my hoe now. I see you choosing a pimp. I need a snow bunny like you on my team. I kno your lil freaky ass luv to fuck, and you fucking and sucking for free! It's time to charge them tricks and cash Daddy out—"

"So—like you're trying to pimp me out, huh? You're crazy as hell!" Miley said, bubbly, cutting Twan off.

"Bitch, what you think ya BFF been doing. She my starting number-one hoe right now! My own cuzzin!"

"OMG! Whoa, I knew y'all was too close for comfort. Jill, you're turning tricks now for your cousin. OMG—You got to walk me through this shit!" Miley said in disbelief.

"Damn it, Shelly, why you think I picked your slutty ass up for? To introduce you to Twan. Now, let's have fun and get paid for it. STOP being a SpongeBob SquarePants and get loose as a goose, bitchhh!" Jill snapped, trying to get her BFF Shelly in line. Then Jill saw Miley look up.

"Like a red nose—And she gonna shake it—Like a red nose…" Sage da Gemini hit single beat hard through the club. Twan saw the crowd forming a circle, then project d-boys throwing racz up. He couldn't see much of the show, but it was drifting toward his way like a tornado twister.

Twan threw six racz ova at his pimpin' partner and said, "Pimp—Chuchh!" His pimp partner threw ten racz and greeted him back, "Chuchhh P!" as he chunked up the deuces as P's do. On each side of the V.I.P. tables, the racz laid dead on the floor. Neither pimp parties touched the colorful big faces. They looked at the money like it was dirt because it touched the ground.

Twan and his pimp partner looked up toward the crowd. A redbone was clapping and shaking her ass like a red-nose pit. All Twan saw was cakes hanging out her tiny half skirt. Then he saw her whole bare pussy as she tooted over. That's why the crowd was over her nasty ass. They saw and smelt pussy! He continued to watch the show as her bare pussy kept flirting and winking at him. Miley and Jill just looked at the nasty light-skinned bitch showing up every hoe in the place, man or no man. It didn't matter. Miley noticed the scandalous bitch dancing was trying to get Twan's undivided attention, and it was working. She felt jealous when she saw his eyes glued to her.

Twan noticed the bitch's face when she turned her head sideways finally while she twerked something. He spit the rosé back into the bottle. His eyes zoomed in. Yes, it was NEESE! Damn, he couldn't believe this hoe, and she had gotten thicker over the weeks. She surprised him, especially after all those times he hit that Creole ass.

As the song went off, Neese began to pick up stacks off the floor that the project niggas were throwing. Some of the project niggas were smacking her juicy booty with rubber band stacks, and others were grabbing and squeezing her ass. Neese didn't care. They'd paid for it.

All she was doing was looking Twan directly in the eyes, trying to see if she got to him or if he was going to choke her out in front of the whole club. She was waiting for a reaction from him. She did know he wasn't dumb enough to go to the County Jail again tonight. She had to admit he was shining and stunting over there in the V.I.P.

section.

She tipped the bouncer to let her in the V.I.P. section. He gladly obliged her. She mean-mugged Jill and some little scrawny white girl Twan had right next to him. She still pursued Twan with all the cash in front of her.

Twan saw Neese walking up with all that crumpled-up money. He couldn't believe the bitch. He shook his head at her, trying to be nonchalant, but he was on fire inside. He wanted to crack the dumb bitch upside the head with both rosé bottles.

"Heyy, Pa! Here goes some money for you. The root of all evil and which you love so damn dearly more than life itself. NE-wayz, Twan, I'm your wifey, and every bitch ain't meant to sell her ass for you or cash you out! Nigga, I love you and forever, gonna be ya day-one bitch and first love before you even considered yourself a PIMP!"

"Neese—BITCH! Don't you ever come up in here fronting on my pimpin' and tryna embarrass me in front of the whole club and my hoes. STOP stalking me and leave before I call security. I'm a catch a case fuckin' wit cha bald-headed ass!" Twan yelled as he cut Neese off.

"Please… Nigga, everybody know I'm ya hoe, bitch, wifey, boo, and whatever else ya want to call it. Nigga, I could have any one of these niggas in here right now, but I choose ya ratchett no-good ass! And Jill, fuck you, nasty bitch. That's ya own cousin, hoe! You think I'm a let cha get away with stealing my man, huh? How long I been knowing you—ugghh! And who's the lil white bitch, Twan? So, you got you a lil snow bunny now too, huh? Her skinny ass ain't gonna make you no damn real money. Niggas like thick bitches. You in Baton Rouge, baby!" Neese said with her thick Creole accent as she scorched Jill and Miley with her piercing eyes.

Twan snapped and jumped up, then grabbed the rosé bottle and swung, missing Neese's head from her flinching. Jill quickly jumped up too and grabbed Twan's arm, saying, "Twan, no!"

Miley scrambled out the way, screaming in shock. She thought Twan was crazy and was going to kill Neese's dumb, drunk ass. Twan spit hard on Neese's face. Neese went berserk and started kicking and swinging wildly. She caught Jill with a blow to the back of her head, dropping her instantly to the floor. Then she kicked Twan in his left ball, dropping him to the ground and leaving him crouched down, holding his nuts, trying to catch his breath and breathe. Miley jumped up and ran out the V.I.P. as the bouncers rushed Neese and carried her out back. They were about to 86 Neese from the establishment permanently. Twan finally mustered up some energy to get up off his knees. He swore he was going to beat the shit out of that bitch Neese soon as he ran into her again. His pimp partner just shook his head from the other V.I.P. table.

Miley ran back into the V.I.P. to help Twan and her BFF. She saw that hoes were throwing themselves at Twan and how much everyone at the packed club respected him and admired him. She saw he was known and popular, a somebody. Now, she wanted to be down for him. She never had so much attention or was the center of attention by black folks in her life. She felt important and alive for once in her life. She mattered. Twan had affected her. She hoped he wasn't mad at her for running out on them, but she couldn't fight and had never been through anything like that in her life. She wanted to make it up to him by deep throating him all night.

Twan pushed Miley's ass off him as he sat back. The female waitress brought them two more bottles of rosé. Twan asked her was it on the house? The waitress shook her head no and pointed at the V.I.P. table that had four out-of-town niggas from Detroit, throwing up deuces to Twan. Twan signaled them over with a head nod.

Miley sat quietly and looked at her BFF, Jill. She watched the four strangers come over to their table and shake Twan's hand. The one guy with the most ice on was the one whispering to Twan. He was short, about 5'7", with a long beard and a mohawk, and fat with a baller gut. She heard them calling him Big Pun.

Then she saw him nod his head and keep grinning. He handed Twan some large stacks of money still with the bank bands on it. It looked like it could've been at least ten grand to her. *OMG!* she thought.

The short fat guy came up to Miley and reached his hand out to her and nodded his head for her to come on with him. She was nervous as hell and looked over at Twan. She didn't know what she was supposed to do.

Jill got up and went up to the tall, dark-skinned one and wrapped her arms around him, then took his partner by the hand and walked off with both the strangers. Miley thought she was crazy and very bold.

Twan said, "It's all good. Big Pun gonna take good care of you and make sure you come back safe."

Miley cracked a bashful smile and extended her hand out to the short fat guy. At that point, she knew she was about to engage in some type of wild drunken orgy.

Later that night, they popped white Molly pills and sipped on Cîroc. Miley had never sucked and fucked so much in her life. Her jaws, pussy, and ass were sore like a real whore. She must've made every nigga cum two to three times, at least. Jill just sat there getting gangbanged, enjoying every bit of it. Miley was happy as hell when Twan pulled up at the Doubletree to get them around 11 a.m. the next morning.

The girls were quiet the whole way to Mama Lela's crib. He knew his hoes got dragged down through there. He could tell by Miley's face she thought that those niggas were Energizer bunnies how they fucked and tag-teamed them into the wee hours of the morning. Those Detroit niggas were trying to get their money's worth out of their asses. He had planned to start Miley out at one date at a time, but when big racz call on deck, he got to answer. It's like supply and demand, but more like a sex service. What better way than to turn her out? That's precisely what she was, freshly turned-out, new game, and brand-new merch. Twan grinned as he pulled up in the driveway.

"Unt-uhh… Hell nawh, Twan. Now, who the dirty trailer-trash white bitch you dragging into my house now? And then Jill, ya nasty trifling ass—I already told you that you're not welcomed here in my house anymore. What's the matter with you, disrespecting me and ya mama, girl? You acting all ratchett, and ya white peeps ain't raised you like that. What happened to Neese, Twan? Now she gonna be ya baby mama and wife one day. Not ya cousin, boy!" Mama Lela said with venom.

"Mama, damn—why u always hating on a pimp! I'm ya son and you a bona fide hoe, too. What you doing here, anyway? I haven't seen you since our last argument about Jill's hot ass," Twan replied in an ill tone.

"Boy, you know I'm here for some dope! Now give me a hundred for 36 dollars. And don't say you don't got it either—"

"Bye, Mama! Get ya ass out of here! You know I stopped selling dope, and you only come to me with that chump change. I'm on to you!" Twan yelled.

CHAPTER 6: Da Ratchetts

"Her pistol go bang-bang…BOOM-BOOM….Chop-chop! Her pistol go—" Twan snapped out of his slumber. He wiped the slobber from his drooling lip, then sat up and sucked his teeth. He was pissed off that he had messed up his Versace sheets. He hated it when he went too hard and drooled all over himself like a damn fool. He spent ten racz on that Versace bed set.

Twan couldn't get that melody out his head. It was like he heard a ringtone repeat over and over in his head. He leaned off his bed and fired up the half a blunt he had in the shot glass he used as an ashtray.

Jill and Miley were already out of the house. Twan looked at the clock that read 3:14 p.m. He needed a drink just to think. He felt like going to a strip joint to get his mind right and think like the laws of attraction to knock another bitch because he wasn't a two-hoe pimp. He needed at least two more hoes. A total of 40 toes down was more his style. He had to think of a master plan and a new method. These hoes in BR weren't choosing fast enough. Maybe it was time to evaluate his game or switch his style up and pop his five P's harder? He didn't know but was undoubtedly about to find out.

He had Jill bringing home at least a stack a night. And Miley was catching more dates and all online with her own profile accepting company, companionship, and donations. The only problem was she was becoming more of a pill head. Jill was drinking more alcohol, too. But Twan didn't care if them hoes popped and drank their lives away. He'd find another hoe to replace them, cousin or not! Fuck 'em all! He didn't have a loving bone in his body, only pimp bones with swagged-out pimp juice.

Twan put on a Hugh Hefner maroon silk robe with some black smiley-face silk boxers. He had slid on his Gucci loafs with no socks, showing his ashy ankles. He jumped in the Caddy rental and smashed downtown BR, right to a hole-in-the-wall ratchett strip joint.

Twan put out his sticky Kush blunt, popped a perk 30, and was ready to percolate. He entered Lipstixx and ordered a double shot of Henny straight without the rocks.

As he sat down, he immediately noticed this gorgeous redbone on center stage that had all eyes on her as she p-popped upside down on a handstand against the pole like a pro. Twan knew she couldn't be from BR, shaking it like that. She was twerking something for real. *Damn!* He had to get a better view of the bright bitch.

He went to the stage and noticed the bitch was indeed a new face to BR and young. She barely looked legal, like she was 18, maybe 19 the most, but not a day over. He noticed all her tatts. She had N.O. tatt on both her ass cheeks. A big old N on her left cheek and the O on her right cheek both done in Old English prison-style letters. Then she had N.O.L.A. tatt on her left upper shoulder, an exotic tramp stamp, and an outline of the state of Louisiana that read "Da Boot."

"Her pistol go BOOM-BOOM! BANG-BANG! Pop-Pop!" ASAP Rocky's single rang out through Lipstixx, and Twan snapped back into consciousness. The perks already were in his blood system. Then it hit him. That's where he heard that song this morning. That's what rhythm he had in his head and woke up hearing. It was destiny. This was his next hoe. Then he felt his dick rock up.

She turned around to walk off stage after she picked up two dozen ones from shaking her moneymaker and showcasing her little tricks. She had uncut talent, but Twan was about to turn her on to some of this pimpin'.

She had hazel eyes, light freckles, fluffy thick pink lips with dimples, with diamond-studded implants in them. Twan also noticed her diamond piercing directly under her bottom lip and a two-diamond dangling navel ring. She walked straight up to him with her ones in hand and wrapped her arms around his neck. She stood 5'5 in 6-inch stilettos.

"What's happening, baby! I see you bling-blinging in this bitch, and you looking at me like you want me and like what you see. Huh, niggah? Do you wanna lap dance? It's 25 dollars, tho!" she said with a rich New Orleans accent that turned him on despite how BR don't like or get along with N.O., even hoes. Pimpin' Twan wasn't trying to hear any of those city-to-city, hood-to-hood beefs.

"Say, check this out. I love what I see! I'm Gucci on the lap dance, but ya right. I do want cha, tho. You so much better than this place. How about we go to my spot on the Southside, where I can straight lace and show you some real things?" Twan replied in a stern tone.

"Awwhh, listen to you trying to mac! I see what this is. You wanna fuck this, huh? Well, I charge for all that, but you can't say shit 'cause I got a crazy dude. My man is a straight lunatic and will kill us both if you got a big ol' mouth. That's why we out here now, 'cause he found out I was selling pussy to all the local ballers and some of the ones he sold big dope to. He took me in when I was 15 years old, and my Mama was strung out and loaded on that needle! Stick around here till 3 o'clock. That'll give us time to play, but you got to get me back here at 5 o'clock when I get off 'cause my dude will be here to pick me up and looking for sure," she said in a skeptical tone with a hint of play as she looked at him mischievously.

"So, you a sneaky hoe, huh? Why you just don't leave that crazy dude and spread ya wings and fly right into a pimp's arms? You meant to sell pussy, not dancing for chump change and getting pimped on from 3 to 4 different angles. Tip da bar, da place, da D.J., and then ya nigga get his fee, too, just from you shaking all night in heels. I need you on my team, and you'd fit in my stable nice. You the missing piece. I got a snow bunny and a half-breed bitch. You can be my redbone from the N.O.—"

"Nawh, nigga. I don't know about all that crazy pimp shit. A bitch ain't trynna do all dat shit and be out chere like dat either. That's why we left N.O. in the first place. I'm just young, wild, and going through some thangs. I'm just trynna get out that boring hotel room, have some fun, and get mines all at the same time. So, if you down, meet me out front at 3 p.m., baby. Now, I gotta get back to work and work these tricks and tables!" she said as she winked at him and walked away with her cash in hand. Twan saw her peek back at him as she switched her ass hard, right before she sat on a Mexican's lap. Twan's lips puckered in madly as he showed his two ratchett gold fangs.

He bled the bar tough and tipping the bartender big, trying to impress the young bitch dancing. She wasn't impressed and knew Twan was still trying to stunt in front. If only Twan knew who her dude was. He had more heroin-smack than man.

Around three, she came up to Twan and told him to meet her out back. Twan told her for sure but wanted to know her name.

"Baby—they call me Diamond Cutz… 'cause I got all these sexy curves with a size 20-inch waist! They stunting like diamond cutz. Also, my crazy fiend mama named me Diamond before the Rihanna song. Now, let's go, baby!" Diamond Cutz explained in a seductive voice, hinting that she was ready to get down for her New Orleans crown.

Twan looked at her gold grill with crushed diamonds, all open-face crowns. It was that New Orleans butter gold. Twan called it that pirate gold because it looked bright like 18k. Then he noticed her tiny waist and real hourglass figure. She had goldilocks. Her dreads were shoulder length. As she swayed her ass, Twan's dick got stiff. He had to hold that motherfucker to calm his aching dick down.

Twan pulled the rental up in the back of Lipstixx, and Diamond Cutz was waiting with her black Chanel bag. Twan was curious if she had her money in there or back in her locker.

"This that sauce, this that dressing, Che-fa-che! God bless ya," 2Chainz Ft. Drake was beating in the rental.

"Ooweee, that's my song right there, baby!" Diamond Cutz said as she grinded on the passenger seat.

Twan saw her getting it and freaking his front seat. He loved her sexy-ass New Orleans accent. He just thought she was a true freaky hoe. But after today she through dancing. He asked her where did she learn to dance like that at? And learn all those little fancy tricks? She told him she used to strip at She She's in the N.O. with a fake I.D. and had to learn how to compete with the vet hoes. They smoked on some purp and popped two more perk 30's.

Diamond Cutz saw the raggedy-ass house Twan pulled up to and knew he wasn't getting any real money. He wasn't pimpin' hard. It looked like a trap house. She knew what time it was. She was about to try to break Twan for all his cash and his bling-bling and give to her dude. Fuck this wannabe Iceberg Slim pimp ass nigga. It was on. She loved to get her some dick and money at the same damn time. She would get her fix and get paid like her name was cashing out.

Twan pulled up to his Mama Lela's crib, happy that Miley and Jill were still out strong, getting his dough all day long. He was about to change this hoe's whole life. By the time he got done with her, they were going to be calling that bitch platinum baguettes. They went into the crib. Diamond Cutz looked around and asked could she use his bathroom to freshen up? Twan took her to his bathroom in his room.

The perks had her clammy, and she was wet as ever, maybe because of the two pills. She and her dude don't do scripts, just straight street-made drugs. It wasn't Ecstasy, but she was feeling it do the trick. She got in the bathroom and looked around and saw all the girly items everywhere. *Twan must live here with his B.M.,* she thought. *Oh well, I ain't trying to break up a happy home, but I'm about to throw this hot ass pussy back on his ass.* She looked down at her iPhone and knew she had to be quick to bust a move and be back to work before her dude came up there tripping and trying to shoot some shit up again. She looked at her face in the mirror and wiped her clammy forehead. She pulled her dreads back in a ponytail, then washed her face. She quickly went through her Chanel bag and pulled out her L'Oréal lipstick. She sat on the toilet, spread her vaginal lips, and slowly inserted the lipstick in her canal, then began to make her vaginal muscle contract tightly around it until the whole lipstick pushed out slowly, then jumped in Twan's shower and used the Peaches and Crème Bed, Bath and Beyond body wash. This was one of her tricks. It was like she was doing Kegels at Lamaze classes like she was pregnant. She cracked a devilish smirk as she washed off and massaged her swollen clitoris.

Twan was on the bed, trying to knock this Asian and white bitch on Instagram. He had been on her ass for three days now when he was interrupted by the shower running. Damn, he wished this New Orleans bitch would hurry up because he was ready to put his mac down. He hurried up and sniffed a line of Ecstasy. It burnt like a motherfucker as the red Mac One drained down the back of his throat. He had to be on his Bay Mac-a-Bitch shit! Fuck that! She was about to go. A real pimp ain't about to hear, "No!" She was hoeing like a renegade out-of-pocket hoe. It was his job to put her right back in pocket just like he had to do with Jill.

Twan's head started spinning fast suddenly. He took a swig of Miley's extra-dry gin and yipped his mouth from the nasty burning fire taste. He was still dizzy as hell. He tried his best to focus. Then he saw Neese's Instagram video stream.

"Hello—Twan! Well, Daddy, I'm not ever too mad at cha too long. I just can't stand them hoes and ya cuzzin skanky in-breed ass. Twan, I love you, niggah, and this pussy is busted wide open for you, soaking soppy wet! So, when you ready to grow up and leave that bullshit street life and all that stupid ass pimpin' alone, come home! Right to ya first love, niggah. Them hoes ain't got shit on ya Creole bitch. Look at this phat wet pussy. Now come get these thongs off ME!" Neese recorded.

Twan had to admit she was looking good, but she didn't respect his pimpin' and wanting him to pimp or send her ass. His thoughts were cut off soon as Diamond Cutz came out of the bathroom asshole naked with beads of dripping water on her that made her glisten and shine bright like the diamond that she was. He had to bag this bad gutta bitch now.

She proceeded to walk toward Twan. She did a full spin-around twice and asked Twan if he liked what he saw. Twan nodded; he was speechless. Then she asked if he wanted what he saw. He nodded yes again! Twan couldn't believe he froze straight up—Damn, what got into him? He was a horny dick! She noticed the bulge in his pants and freed his manhood massaging it and then manipulating it with her diamond-studded tongue ring, flicking tricks all around his head. Twan just grabbed her ass cheeks. They were so, so soft but not sloppy soft.

She began to bop her head up and down on Twan's long shaft as his eyes rolled in the back of his head.

"O-o-hh, fuck, bitch! Damn, u-uggh-ghh! Damn, you got me cumming already. You ain't no joke, a straight natural!" Twan said as he unexpectedly jolted twice. Then he felt his dick grow an inch and extra hard as she did another trick, flickering her tongue at the very tip point of his head. Twan let out a manly moan as he grunted and clenched his ass tight, rising off the bed.

Diamond Cutz pushed his chest back down as she told him to relax and forced him to take more of her super head. She knew he was super sensitive right then, and she was on the verge of working her New Orleans voodoo on him.

She straddled him and grabbed his manhood and began to swirl it around on her phat clit, then up and down of her wet, warm crevices. She saw Twan's dreamy sex eyes. She already had his nose wide open. Then she paused briefly; she couldn't tease Twan anymore. She was ready for some dick!

"Baby, where ya Magnums at? I'll get them, relax. I'm 'bout to ride this big dick, Chere!" Diamond Cutz said in a provocative, sexy tone.

Twan jumped up and started tearing through his drawers and looking all around in his closet till he realized he was shit out of luck and fucked! He fell back on the bed with a hard dick, defeated. He sighed out a deep breath, knowing Jill and Miley had all the condoms with them. He knew Diamond Cutz was about to get loose, too, and wanted to perform magic tricks on his dick!

She climbed back on top of him again and proceeded to tease them both as she whispered in his ear softly, "I see you want this ass and feel ya dick jumping for me! It's too bad I only fuck my dude raw—Sorry for you, baby. You should've been on top of ya A-game, boy!" As Diamond Cutz withdrew from his ear, she flicked her tongue ring across the bottom of her gold teeth. Then she got up and began to dance seductively to the 2Chainz and Drake "No Lie!"

"Bitch, I don't neva eva fuck no stray hoe without a rubber, especially a sneaky lil out-of-pocket down-low hoe like you. You fucking for recreation use and the thrill! You a cum freak. Even tho you may get paid, it's still rules to this shit! Now, come choose up with a real pimp! Fuck that crazy nigga. Let's build a million-dollar empire!" Twan popped as he watched her move her body like a snake, a dirty wind.

That did it right there. Was it something Twan said that set her off? Something deep inside her had been triggered. She wanted to challenge Twan. Today she was about to break all rules of engagement. She rushed Twan like a red nose pit and dove on top of him. She grabbed his dick, spread herself, and sat down slowly as she leaned back for Twan to get an eyeful of her pretty pussy.

Twan felt her tight, wet, warm gushy pussy. Damn, she had some super fire! She was a triple threat. Bad dime piece, little waist, cute face, good head, and a bomb shot of cott! They started fucking like wild animals, each trying to conquer the other's body until they both came at the same time. Twan pulled out and finished skeeting all over her pink-nippled titties. She rubbed it in, then licked her dripping sticky crème-filled titties. Twan couldn't believe how she could take dick with her shallow tight snatch. She made some of the craziest fuck faces ever! She had a peculiar moan; it wasn't too loud like she was faking it. It was more passionate, and she was vibing with him. Her moans became more high-pitched the deeper Twan hit the bottom of her snatch until they both came.

She rubbed Twan and curled up with him tightly until they both passed out, snoring. They put each other to bed for real, though.

BOOM! "Ohh, hell nawh—No! Daddy, who is this bitch? Naw! Huh? We don't need no stray lil alley cat ratchett-ass hoes!" Jill yelled when she saw Twan sprawled out naked in the bed with some light-skinned, tatted-up dread-head bitch with her arms across him.

Twan snapped out of his slumber with his dick still hard. He already wanted another shot of that fire and desire she guarded between her legs. Jill noticed his stiff dick and grew angrier and more envious.

Diamond Cutz jumped up and sucked her teeth as she reached for her phone, checking for the time. It was 4:48 p.m.! She only had 12 minutes to get dressed, cleaned up, and to be back at Lipstixx before her crazy dude popped up, acting a straight donkey!

"Shit! C'mon, please—I gotta go. I don't got time for all this drama. I got drama of my own. Sorry, but I can't see you no more or do this no more! I mean you can come see me dance at the club, but that's it, okay? Just forget this ever happened. Them perks had me horny as a goat. Now please drop me off. And girl, please...I don't want cha man. I could have him if I want him. I got a dude, so get on with all that riff-raff!" Diamond Cutz said as she put on her G-string and pasties, then grabbed her Chanel bag to put all the gold glitter back on her that Twan had fucked off her. Jill noticed all the gold sprinkles all over Twan's dumb trifling ass, looking like a damn fool and a simp, not a pimp! Twan was quiet and knew he was tender dicking off them pills all horny dick. He hurried up and floored it to Lipstixx, running stop signs and a few red lights through BR.

When they arrived at Lipstixx, Diamond Cutz got low in the front seat, so her dude couldn't see her and told Twan to drive straight to the back. She was so shook that it had him paranoid, too.

He looked around the parking lot and saw this '72 dunk with New Orleans Saints symbols all over it. It was black and gold, the same New Orleans Saints color, with limo tint, sitting high on some all-black tires with gold trimming. It looked vicious. Whoever her nigga was, he was getting dough for real. Twan pushed to the back slowly. He wanted the bitch out his rental, too. He could see how the nigga was pussy whipped over his young bitch. He didn't have time for no love triangle type shit because someone always ended up hurt in those. He'd catch up to the little ratchett bitch. Besides, it looked like her dude had something off the *Sons of Guns* arsenal in that dunk if he was sitting on a dunk worth $75k easy just off all the customized work.

She slammed the door, mad at him. Twan screamed out, "Bitch!" She turned around and flicked him smooth off with both her middle fingers. Twan smirked as he lit up the half purp blunt. He drove out and saw a half-window crack of the dunk with smoke blowing out and a row of gold slugs glowing. It was the same gold as Diamond Cutz, that N.O. 18k butter shit.

Right then, Twan knew it was time to step up out of the rental and get him a new whip and his own crib. He couldn't be pimpin' living with his Mama and off the land. One day his ratchett hoes were going to wake up, as every hoe does sooner or later. *Stay sleep, hoe, and bring pimpin' his dough!* Twan thought with a grin.

CHAPTER 7: Shine

The past few weeks had been crazy for Twan ever since he ran into Goldilocks at Lipstixx. He went back a few times on Tuesdays to see if he could catch Diamond Cutz at work. One Tuesday, he stayed all day. He figured her old man must've caught her up and handcuffed the bitch to another joint or city. Who knows?

Miley had been acting up lately, too. Her ass was becoming more ratchett as the days moved on. He didn't know if it was BR effect or just her being around a bunch of all black folks. He had her doing escorts downtown with all those high-end businessmen in suit and ties. She would drink and pop pills all day to drive her pain away. Twan didn't care. He never sexed her ass again, and she felt some kind of way about it. So far, he had 23 racz out of her ass escorting and being online. She'd catch way more dates than Jill. He didn't allow Jill to call her family. He didn't want them spitting that venom in her ear, telling her how she didn't need to sell her body and how much they loved her, that Twan was a low-life scum pimp that was using and abusing her. Twan had to keep her brainwashed and make her feel important and needed at all costs and times. Therefore, he allowed her and Jill to sleep in the bed with him after they came home and washed their funky asses.

Mama Lela walked through the front door, looking cat-raggedy and smoked the fuck out. She looked like she was on her last leg and breath of life, too. Twan felt sorry for her because she was still his mama— even if she was a hoe and a crackhead. So what? She was blood, and she was loved. He didn't hold too much against her beside his older brother's death and his little brother getting killed at the park. He peeled her off some big faces. He didn't care if she smoked it up or not, as long as she enjoyed it and felt the love. Even she was shocked.

"Damn, son! That's what I'm talking about, son. You know ya mama loves you, boy. You my only son I have left. Even tho you soft and not a gangsta or D-boy like ya brother was—You still pimp of the year—pimp on! I really don't want you moving out, Twan, away from ya mama, boy. Stay," Mama Lela pleaded happily as she counted the six hundred-dollar bills and thinking about her crack pipe.

"Pssh… Please, Twan, why you give that crackhead my hard-earned money? She didn't suck and fuck for it! Lay her down on her back and tell her to spread her smelly legs for her own dough. CRACKHEAD BITCHHH!" Jill said slickly with a piercing gaze at Mama Lela and Twan ass.

"Please, you trifling heifer! I been wrote ya mama and told her about ya nasty hot ass. Twan, I hope you don't take ya nasty-ass cousin with you. Where my girl Neese at? That's my daughter-in-law right there. Jill don't even cook for you. What type of pimp has hoes that can't cook for you? All they bring you is cold carry-out. And Lord knows that skinny-ass white girl can't cook either. Matter of fact, Jill, take her back to that white family with you that you came from, too! BYE, BITCH! Twan, I'm gone. I got Johnny Lee waiting on me. You kno he don't come in no more ever since you pistol-whipped him with that shotgun and knocked his teeth out. That's gonna be my husband. Twan, he gonna marry me soon!" Mama Lela said in a fast tone like crack was on her mind as she rolled her sunk-in eyes at Jill and fidgeted with the door as she walked out the door.

Twan had found a nice house for lease on the north side of BR. It was a 3-bedroom, 2-bath for $1,200 a month. Then he put five racz down on a 2014 brand-new Cadillac EXT truck. His note was $600 a month, with $500 for full coverage insurance. That was all in his cousin Jill's name. Twan didn't have any credit. He didn't even know what credit was.

Twan spent the next few weeks tricking his Escalade out. He had it painted a champagne color with champagne tint with Gucci print on the bottom and on his leather interior. He had six screens in it with two 15-inch subs and four 12-inch subs. He sat it slick on some 26-inch dubs, all chrome floaters.

He had Mama Lela pimpin' out his new crib to make it look more like a player's pad like he was a straight bachelor. He had an all-black leather living room set and stainless-steel appliances with Gucci bed sets. He was shining bright like an all-star.

Twan popped up in his EXT truck stunting at Lipstixx to get a drink and to think. When he sat down, he saw Diamond Cutz come to the center stage.

It was like déjà vu all over again. She looked like a million-dollar hoe. All he saw was dollar signs straight up. Diamond Cutz was caught off guard and surprised to see Twan again, too. She had her eyes on him her whole dance routine. Tricks were still making it rain, throwing stacks, trying to be the lucky chosen one that night. However, for some reason, she wanted Twan and wanted to play all over again. She had been getting wet for no reason lately out of nowhere. Twan had her juices flowing more than ever down there. She was hot in the ass and started gyrating like she was horny as a toad. Twan just looked more mature and like a man. Something happened new to him over the past few weeks. He was shining with a glow. And it wasn't just from all his ice either. She was curious and wanted to jump right off the stage and onto his lap, then put on a real show and freak him in front of everybody. She didn't care at all. Then she thought about taking him by the hand and blowing this joint.

Twan looked away, thinking, *Fuck this childish-ass hoe.* He didn't have time for her ass or them high school games. He summoned his hand for another double shot of Cîroc and tipped the bartender another dub.

He watched Diamond Cutz come from backstage ten minutes later. She had gold glitter sprinkled all over her, walking up to the bar. Twan pulled out the 20 racz he had in both his front pockets. He had his maroon silk shirt half-buttoned up to show his icy chain hanging low.

Diamond Cutz got a bottle of water and tipped the bartender a dub, too. She saw Twan counting colorful big-face hundreds. He looked so sexy with his silk shirt open, even though he was scrawny with a bird chest.

"So damn, Twan, you gonna keep shining me off or say something to a bitch? Huh?" she said with her thick N.O. accent, annoyed.

"Shit…I ain't got shit to say, bitch. It ain't gonna be no laying around and playing around—Nawh, it's gonna be a whole lot of getting down and staying down, bitch!" Twan snapped.

"Pssh…Whatever, Twan. You just don't understand, baby! Now can we get out of here, please? I don't care. Let's just go somewhere. I'll give you money—if that's what you want, cuz it don't mean shit to me. My dude out of town right now, and he gots me caged up in the hotel room by myself all day long," she replied sadly as she sucked her teeth.

Twan looked at Diamond Cutz and noticed she had a bruised split lip, and she seemed broken-spirited. He knew what that meant; she was tired of her old man and yearned for some of this pimpin'. He snatched her up right there in her work stage college student outfit. The manager yelled at Twan and tried to call for Diamond Cutz, telling her don't do it, and they don't turn no tricks there. It's not a Vegas brothel. He was pissed and threw the stale cigar out of his mouth.

Diamond Cutz trailed behind Twan in her six-inch clear stilettos. He led her to his custom champagne-colored Escalade truck on 26's.

She was surprised and digging what she was seeing, especially his Gucci trim. He helped her into the truck. Twan heard someone yell, "Owwee…Uugghh…Pimpin' snatched N.O.'s bitchhh!"

But Twan didn't give a fuck! He hated when niggas handcuffed and captain slave these maggot ass hoes. He hopped in and pushed his remote start by the keychain.

Diamond Cutz saw the big screen come to life as she rubbed the Gucci and leather front seat and dash. It had that brand-new car smell. She was highly impressed. Then the system beat her back in. She asked Twan to cut it down, please, so she could explain everything to him, and Twan complied as he smashed out the parking lot and leaned back like a true pimp! He felt like a million-dollar pimp with a million-dollar hoe. It was a wrap, Jack!

She told Twan to take her to the hotel at first, so she could clip her dude's stash. It was one of his many stashes. He kept a little here and a little there but spread around everywhere.

She told him how her dude would go back to New Orleans and do the drug deal. Then, she'd go on the Greyhound with all the cash to N.O. and come back the next day with all the heroin and bricks in her carry-on bags so nobody jacked her and the dogs wouldn't hit on it from the bottom of the Greyhound with the rest of the passengers' luggage. Twan just listened and nodded while hitting the Cali Humboldt County Kush. He told her she already knew what she had to do. She smiled, then got sick to her stomach. She couldn't cross her crazy-ass dude, but she wanted to start all over fresh with Twan. She'd rather give her money to Twan than to her dude because he hustled and didn't need it or appreciate it. She never even got a kiss, let alone a "thanks, baby."

Twan pulled up to the hotel suite, and Diamond Cutz rushed up the steps holding her stomach, then she hurled all over the place. Twan didn't even get out to help her. He was more worried her crazy nigga might pull up and start shooting up his new truck.

She went into the hotel suite for 15 minutes. She took a shower, put on a long one-piece velvet body catsuit with no bra or panties. She came back out with close to $7,500 that she gave to Twan. Twan knew that nigga was truly balling if these almost eight stacks were only pinching him. He looked at her pale face and asked if she was Gucci. She shook her head and asked Twan to roll down the window; she needed some fresh air. Twan put the blunt out and let both windows down. About two minutes later, she wanted the windows back up. Twan asked the bitch why she was having hot flashes and asked the bitch did she have AIDS. Some of them loose N.O. bitches be marching around there with that package, too. She shook her head. Twan stopped by the 7-Eleven to buy her a 7Up and him some blunts and a bottle of cognac. She ran over to the Walgreens across the street. They were on the Northside. She didn't know her way around, but Twan told her the new crib was around the corner.

They pulled up to Twan's crib three blocks away in a nice area of BR. It seemed like a working-class neighborhood without no gangs, fiends, or hoes around, a quiet home-feeling neighborhood. Twan saw her digging the new spot as he pulled up in his spotless driveway and thought *Pimpin' ain't dead. Fuck what they said!* He was one of the P's keeping it alive.

She loved the inside of Twan's crib and asked him if she could stay there with him for the next couple of days so she wouldn't be solo in that cramped-up hotel suite. Twan told her it was her house, too, and she was welcome to come home when she was ready to get with some of this real pimpin' and get down for her crown like his other hoes doing. She excused herself, went into the bathroom with the Walgreens bag. She waited for two minutes for the Fast Response E.P.T. test. She prayed two lines didn't come up. Then she walked out of the bathroom, feeling happy. She was ready to put on a super freak show for Twan and ride his dick for two whole days straight.

Twan didn't have time to babysit but this little tenderoni bitch was bad, just ratchett as hell. He fucked her five times during those two days. Her pussy was sweet, and he knew better, but he kept telling himself this was the last time he tender-dicked this bitch.

The first night Jill and Miley came home, Jill started a hot mess catfight, and they both jumped Diamond Cutz. Well, they tried. Diamond Cutz grew up fighting ratchett hoes from all over N.O. from high school to her projects in the 9th Ward. She knew how to swing like a nigga. Her crazy-ass old man would beat her ass, but she would still scrap with him with her tiny ass. She was dukin' Miley's and Jill's asses up, banging them two hoes up! She left them both leaking and crying to Twan.

Twan sat back and watched and let them scrap. He was amused and was curious to who would win between her and Neese's crazy Creole ass. Neese had a bit more weight on her and an inch or two taller. So, she might get Diamond Cutz, but Diamond fought with precise aggression.

Miley was pouting hot and jealous because Twan gave Diamond her own room, but Jill and Miley had to share a room like little girls. And they heard every time Twan fucked her because she would rub it in and scream extra hard like he was killing her. It was like an episode of *Housewives of Atlanta*, drama on top of more dramatic drama.

After the two days were over, Twan dropped her back off at the hotel. The girls were relieved. Diamond Cutz' dude came back that night and put her straight on the Greyhound with the re-up cash. She came back that following day as planned on the Greyhound with all the work, then went back to work at Lipstixx, where she met Twan and broke him off. Then fucked up his world.

"Twan, I'm pregnant by you! My dude can't have no kids cuz he got shot, and you know the rest. I went to the doctor, and they said I was about a month pregnant now. I told you to use a rubber, baby—"

POWWW! "Bitch, stop playing hoe! Ya crazy ass ain't pregnant. I can't have kids either, else Neese would've been had two or three kids by me! Please, you just want attention, hoe! I ain't going!" Twan snapped after he backhanded the shit out of her. She held her burning face as a tear glided down her cheek. She told Twan she didn't care but was just letting him at least know he had a child on the way, and it was indeed his because she always used condoms on tricks and her dude can't have kids, period. It was her first time pregnant, and she wasn't leaving her dude for Twan if he was going to do the same thing and abuse her, too.

Then she got up and told Twan goodbye and have a good life. She called a cab back to her dude's spot. Twan just sat there stuck, letting her walk away as he watched her storm out the door. Twan was cold as ice and just shrugged his shoulders as he counted the stacks she clipped from her dude.

Jill and Miley went back to getting that dough, and Twan gave them their own rooms finally. Miley was still a breadwinner by far with her skinny ass. Twan promised her to pay for an ass and titty job so she can be deadlier and make more dough! From Miley to Iggy!

A month later Twan had a knock at his door early in the morning around 5:30 a.m. Miley answered while Twan jumped up, paranoid. It was Diamond Cutz. She came in wheeling two Louis Vuitton luggage. One was full of money and the other full of dope. She licked her old man for 114 racz and six bricks of raw uncut heroin. She left him a note saying she was running away back home to N.O., and she felt this was her cut. Really, she was blowing up too fast, and her little kangaroo pouch started showing. And she knew her dude would kill her dead, so she figured she might as well rob his ass, too. Fuck it. She was going big and was praying Twan would take her in. She hoped it was good enough. She even took his money-counting machine, too. Twan was her baby daddy and the only other person she had in life, not just in BR. Twan woke up to his B.M. moving in with dough and dope. He was paranoid.

CHAPTER 8: Pimpin'

Since Twan had given Miley the other room, Diamond Cutz moved into his room, which caused chaos in the house. Twan had to go out and buy a French bulldog puppy to calm his hoes down. They all fell in love with the vanilla-colored puppy. They treated it like it was a baby. Miley named him Snack because he loved them little PetSmart Puppy Yummy snacks.

He had his hoes back on track despite the new pregnant house member to the stable. Diamond Cutz was just laying around eating up everything and ordering pineapple pizza she kept craving for. Twan loved when she cooked all that gumbo and Louisiana Cajun-style food. He even put on a few pounds in a month with her.

Twan heard his ring back and grabbed Diamond Cutz' Smartphone by accident. He realized it was hers from the diamond rhinestones cover around it. He snatched his up and saw a new number and didn't answer. Then he got a text message. It read:

Twan, so that's how you gonna do a bitch? I see you got you a lil family now and a cute lil puppy dog. LOL! WOW! Nigga, u ain't shit. How u gonna settle down with a ratchett-ass hood rat? Over ya 1st love and the only bitch to hold u down on lockdown in dat raggedy BR County Jail! U all on Instagram shining and Twitter fronting like you pimp of the year. Oh yeah, nigga, u better be careful cuz rumor has it that u snatched some out-of-town nigga bitch from Lipstixx and he saying he gonna bust that pimp nigga head! So, lay low. I still love u for some reason, even though u treat me like shit and drag me thru the mud errtime. Having a baby on me? I told u anything but that. I'm sorry, Pa. I can't forgive 4 dat one. Have a nice life, fool. N please don't come by my Mama's house either. Now she really hates u!!

Twan read Neese's long-ass text. It was more like a tweet novel. He shook his head, wondering how her crazy stalking ass always got his new numbers. This new social media and technology area was crucial. If you have a Twitter account or Instagram, they could get your number.

He didn't give a fuck what Neese was babbling on about. Fuck her and her feelings. She should've got down and played her position. He told her he always believed every bitch had a position to play, especially on his team, which reminded him about his own stable. Fuck the haters and what the rest of BR thought. They weren't paying him or his mortgage and car note.

Right then and there, he had an epiphany. He stood up and snatched Diamond Cutz up and told her it was time for her to get off her ass and back out there. She told Twan never and that she was pregnant with his child, and nobody would want a bloated pregnant hoe! Twan twisted a fist full of hair and pressed his knuckles down in her tender scalp hard. She felt her extra-sensitive scalp throbbing in agony. She thought Twan pulled a handful of dreads out by the roots.

"Bitchh! I don't care if you showing. You still hoe-n and go-n! I put dat on my pimpin'! Regardless my B.M. or not. My son gonna know his Mama was a hoe, and Daddy was a pimp! He gonna be second-generation pimpin'. I let him see it's in his veins and to pimp on! Now, get some hoey shit on, and let's go, hoe! I'm 'bout to drop you off with Jill at the Marriott!" Twan said viciously.

"Baby, what if my dude I robbed sees me? He gonna kill me and ya baby, too! You don't know if it's a boy or not. What if it's a lil gurrl? Then what, pimpin'? You gonna send your daughter, too? Huh? It wouldn't surprise me, nigga, cuz you already sat your own cousin down on the hoe stroll and online. Twan, you a ratchett cold, heartless nigga! You know that, right? You make me sick! I feel like throwing up! What about if I catch something and give ya child something, too, huh? You didn't think about that, fool. I'm not a stupid bitch, Twan. I'm smart; so are Jill and Miley, too. It ain't that we don't know better; it's that we want to please you and keep you happy! We put up with ya shit and having to share you because we choose to, and all love you in some way or another. Dummy! Now let me go get dressed or, excuse me, hoey, as you call it. Boy, I can show you nasty-fuck slutty!" Diamond Cutz replied in a whimpering squeaky tone as she wiped her puffy, pouring red eyes. Twan just shrugged and sparked his blunt French inhaling through his nostrils. He watched her half-naked ass shake as she stormed off to the bathroom to get washed up and put on her best hoe fit.

Twan sprayed his 26's dubs off with Windex, a ratchett hood secret to have them floaters shinning. He was beating that Lil Boosie "Wipe Me Down." He pressed the remote start when he heard Diamond Cutz' stilettos click-clacking, beating her feet on concrete. She had on a transparent see-thru shirt and a diamond-studded G-string that disappeared between her ass cheeks as she switched like she was the bitch! Twan knew she wore the see-thru shirt so they could see her little baby knot. She just looked like she had a slight gut and was getting fat. Little did she know it was going to cause a reverse effect. The tricks loved pregnant, wet warm pussy!

"Heyyy!! Bankroll after bankroll. I like it. Big money!" Twan rapped the Lil Boosie "Bad Azz" lyrics, then helped Diamond in the champagne EXT.

He drove her to the hotel downtown without saying a single word. She grabbed the blunt from pimpin' and hit it deep and long. Twan normally would've backhanded the bitch trying to disrespect his pimpin' in a major way. A bitch better not snatch anything from a pimp! He knew she wanted a reaction out of him. He didn't care if she smoked while she was pregnant. That was on her. If his baby came out with asthma, he was going to beat the bitch ass and choke her out straight up. She kept his blunt and smoked it up. He just sparked another one with a shit-face grin. She wanted to smack the blunt out his mouth.

Twan pulled up to the hotel and went to room 212, giving Jill a surprise visit. Jill was in there laying butt ass naked with her face still in the pillow. The room stank like asshole. Yuck. He could see the K-Y Hers on the nightstand with the phone. It was like 4 hundred-dollar bills next to the K-Y box.

"Bitch, get ya ass up. You got a new bitch to lead. You the head bitch, so show her the routine and where to stash the cash. Give her the Phantom Mace and her own box cutter, too. Make sure y'all got y'all own 12-pack of Magnums, and that's it! Y'all stuck to each other like glue now. So, I don't care if y'all kill each other. Just have my bread. And no robbing y'all tricks. It's too hot and bad for biz. Y'all not street track walkers. Nawh—I could've got a thieving-ass hoe for that if I wanted that, fa sho! Now, who loves you??" Twan said, choppin' and poppin'.

"You do, Daddy!" they replied simultaneously.

"Twan, but she's pregnant. Ain't that bad for the baby? Plus, I don't want her around here with me, sharing my clients. She can get her own clientele, just like Miley, and set her lil ass down on the Southside somewhere, cuz you kno them project niggas will love her ratchett New Orleans ass!" Jill said sassily.

Twan snatched up the four bills off the nightstand and hit the stash up under the hotel box spring, then told Jill don't bring her stank ass home for another two weeks with anything less than 14 stacks, which was at least a stack per day. Then he told Diamond Cutz he didn't want to see her pregnant ass until she had 28 stacks, double what Jill had to do. And he didn't care how long it took. He told them to switch rooms every week and stay together until he decided what motel he wanted to sit Diamond pregnant ass down in, probably somewhere in the suburbs; outskirts of BR. He was thinking a rural area might be good. He fixed his rayon purple long-sleeve shirt, popped his collar in the hotel body mirror in the vanity bathroom as he wiped his nose and sniffed twice, like a pimp that just did a line of sugar bugger. Then he did a pimp strut with his hand dangling and following behind him as he walked out the room, leaving the door wide open.

Jill jumped up asshole naked and yelled, "FUCK YOU, TWAN! MOTHERFUCKER! ASSHOLE!" as she stood out in the hotel hallway naked, carrying on and letting the white girl come out in her half-breed ass. Twan didn't turn around, he just pimped on.

Twan got downstairs and saw that Neese had texted him on his Smartphone, asking for him to please come to her Mama's house to see him and that she didn't know he moved out his Mama Lela's house either. Twan shook his head and knew that this Creole bitch was bi-polar and a straight stalker that wouldn't let him go. You would think he had put some black magic voodoo on her ass.

Twan went to press his remote start and suddenly was struck on the shoulder. Then, he saw a stiletto bounce off his shoulder blade and hit his champagne Escalade truck. He turned around and saw Jill ass, butt naked, still crying and screaming to take his pregnant B.M. with him with another stiletto held high above her head cocked back, ready to launch it at him. He shook his head and told Jill she better not and that she was out of pocket. Then he warned her that they'd call the BR police on them. She didn't care and chucked the other stiletto as hard as a baseball at Twan. Twan flinched and jumped up, moving both his legs like he was double-dutching. He fell against his truck to brace his fall as the Escalade roof caught him. The impact of the stiletto hitting Twan forced him to drop his keys, too. That was the last straw.

This time it was on, and Jill knew it by how fast Twan skipped up the first flight of stairs. She screamed and tried to make it back to the room. Twan clipped her legs, knocking her feet from under her. She took a harsh fall and slid on her chin. Then Twan kicked her square in the ass. He put his foot so square up her ass that she jumped up and flew a couple feet as she yelped like a hurt dog. Jill held her stomach, crying. Diamond Cutz ran out and grabbed Twan, telling him to stop and leave Jill alone before he goes to jail for domestic violence. Twan looked down and noticed he had some brown shit on his shoes. This nasty bitch! He really kicked the shit out of her ass and made her shit on herself. Scary square bitch! He took off both of his shoes and left them there right in the hallway. He looked at Diamond as she helped Jill dumb ass up as she staggered, bubbly.

"And wash ya stinky ass, hoe, fo I cancel ya ass like Nino Brown! Pimpin' got a Kush weed habit!" Twan yelled, going hard and smashing on his bitches.

Jill sat around the whole day, turning down tricks so Diamond Cutz would take over and flat-back while Jill sat and watched her on the other bed. It wasn't until the next day she came back around. She hated Twan for what he did, but more for bringing this pregnant bitch around her, watching her turn tricks and being a tagalong hoe, knowing that they didn't get along. She wanted to have Twan's baby. She didn't care if he was her cousin, because they were way past that point, especially considering how many times Twan had skeeted down her throat and fucked her raw like he loved her. She loved him and been idolizing him since she was young. And this was the thanks she got, stuck with his pregnant bitch.

She went to FuckBuddy.com and put in Baton Rouge surrounding area codes. She told Diamond Cutz to charge all of the dudes that wanted to get down, and that nothing was going down for free if she wanted to be free and not lay dormant in a hotel room forever because 28 racz was a lot to suck and fuck for, especially with these cheap BR tricks trying to give you some streetwalking hoe price. Thirty and forty dollars were crackhead prices; $30 and $40 for everything—head, pussy, and then try to slide it up your ass for free! Jill proceeded to snap Diamond's sexy pictures and create her a profile, then did the same with Fish.com.

Diamond Cutz felt some type of way that Twan had turned around and done her way worse than her old dude. At least he let her leave to go out and strip, then to the mall and shop, but Twan, hell nawh. His greedy, selfish ass wanted to ground her to the hotel room until she gave birth. As the days went on, they were turning tricks, but every time one of their tricks would show up, they'd request special shit like a threesome or to watch them eat each other out or fuck each other. Diamond Cutz didn't care and got down with a few hoes before with her old dude in New Orleans. They just were freaky like that and open, but Jill couldn't stand bumping pussies. She hated Diamond Cutz and fucking with females. Licking pussy and asshole was disgusting to her. She had to refuse a couple of clients because it was just too damn much for her back to back. She wanted her own room back and to get rid of Diamond Cutz. She even thought about killing her ass in her sleep and blaming it on a trick! Why not? She didn't have a criminal record and was a college student. She looked at the box cutter, then Diamond's precious neck. She snapped out of her demonic state and thought about how much harder she had to work to get Twan's dough and meet his quota.

The very next day, Jill went on her period and got a new room, leaving Diamond by herself, warning her not to tell Twan shit. She told her if he does pop up, which she highly doubted, to just say she went to the store for some condoms. Little did Diamond know, Jill nasty ass was still going to turn tricks on her rag. She didn't care and just wanted to make the 14 racz ASAP.

Two weeks went by and neither one of them had earned what Twan set out for them to make, so he left them both in the hotel for two more months. Every month they switched hotels, so Johnny Law didn't send his vice squad running up in there, snatching his bitches up. He only kept Miley around him to cook, clean, and be his little slave, doing whatever he told her to and when. It was better this way for Twan because he didn't have to worry about him tender dicking the little boney snow bunny. She didn't turn him on; he didn't like white girls. They were too plain, dull, with no swagger. He reminded himself to pimp hard.

CHAPTER 9: Astray Hoe

Twan was smashing down the Southside, showing off his 6's, floating past the projects where his older brother got murked. He mumbled, "Rest in peace, Bruh-Bruh. This pimpin' is for you... Sorry I wasn't a gangsta like you and Daddy ass." Then he took a dry swig of the bumpy face gin, his big brother's favorite.

Twan heard his text message vibrating off his front dash. He checked and turned his head and neck sideways like *uughh, who dat?* It was a sex pic of a Brazilian waxed coochie. It was phat as a plum and juicy, gleaming like a peach. He didn't know who sent it but some hoe in BR was choosing though. Then he finally made out the tatt right above her swollen clit. It read: *TWAN'S* in fancy script letters. The thing was the tatt didn't look fresh.

Who da fuck? Twan thought as he scratched his hair and twisted the phone sideways, trying to take another good look at the pic. It was a selfie of all gushing vagina.

His phone started going ham with a hundred new pics and texts. He wanted to cut it off from it exploding. Then he answered his ringtone.

"Hello—"

"Pa...Please don't act surprised. I kno u like the pic, and you see I can still cum fast and hard playing with my thang-thang, thinking of you being up in this throbbing wet-wet, Pa! Do you like my new tatt, Pa? Huh? Cuz it's fa ya. This is Twan's pussy, and every nigga that stick they dick head up in this pussy gonna recognize. So, when you stop being funny, come to my Mama's house and let's have some hard-smashing good make-up sex!" Neese said in a soft horny voice.

Click! Twan hung up on Neese even though he could hear her horny voice yearning for his hook dick to beat that pussy up, down, and all around. He couldn't even lie or hide. She had his dick stiff as a dead dog. He held his dick tight and then massaged his dick head. He was about to go let one off in Miley's tonsils. She would love to do the honors for Daddy and be obliged.

He showed the pic to Snack, and then rubbed Snack's head on the passenger seat and told Snack he'll be able to fuck real soon. Twan planned to breed Snack with another French bulldog because their puppies were going for $2,500 online. The bitches couldn't put little Snack down. It was worse than having a newborn baby. Twan had Snack everywhere he went in BR riding shotgun. Miley had been taking care of Snack and letting him sleep in the bed with her. She would even kiss the dog and let it lick her in the mouth, and Twan would call her a nasty dirty trailer-park ass bitch.

Twan had Miley blow his socks off. She got better in a matter of months. She was officially a bonafide hoe and sucked cock like a pro. She and Jill had been at war lately, and envy played a big part in it. Jill's money was decreasing by the weeks. She wasn't really into it that much no more. She finally realized that Twan didn't love her or feel the same way she did about him. He was just using and abusing her. She would try to put Miley up on G, but Miley would run back and tell Twan every single word. Twan would tell Miley Jill was just hating because she made more dough than Jill. Plus, Jill was mad at the fact that she had to live out of a hotel while Miley lived in the comfort of a house that was all in her name and being paid for with her money that she had to hoe for and get out her ass. Twan knew all the melodrama was going on and didn't care. More hoes, more problems.

He pulled up at the Holiday Inn on the Southside, where he had Diamond Cutz and Jill staying. He went to check bread from both of them. Jill didn't come out, so he told Diamond to go snatch Jill dumb ass's bread up, too, and he didn't have time for her stupid childish games. She was becoming more out of pocket and distant from him. He hated to have to keep beating her ass until she got some act right. Gorilla pimpin' wasn't his style, but he'd smack a bitch up quick, fast, and in a hurry.

He counted Diamond's few stacks. The money was extremely low. Then he counted Jill's stash, and it was low, too. Jill's was low as hell but still double of Diamond's issue.

He got heated, and his nose flared. Twan looked over at Diamond Cutz. Her face had swollen. Her nose looked pudgy, and her stomach was enormous. It was like everything on her had grown, even her gold locks were dropping down past her shoulders now.

"Well, Twan, don't just stare at me, stupid! You know I'm pregnant and showing big time. I'm going on my third term, Twan. Tricks find it disgusting. Then in the morning, I'm sick and throwing up or eating anything I can get my hands on. All I crave is pineapple pizzas and chocolate ice cream and Red Devil hot sauce. It's weird, baby!" Diamond Cutz said in an innocent high-pitched tone.

Twan sat there looking at her and thinking. He was going to tell her to bounce soon as she had the baby. He didn't even think the baby was really his anyway. She had to show him it was. Then she'd be out his life for good.

Twan said, "Naw, that ain't my baby. You way more months pregnant than we knew each other. That yo ole dude baby."

Diamond Cutz shook her head and then rolled her eyes at Twan. "Please, I'm five going on six months pregnant, and I'm pregnant with your twins, a boy and a girl."

She was carrying and eating for two babies. She named them Twan and Twanita. Twan would've known this if he would've come to the doctor with her every month. Her OB/GYN instructed her to go every two weeks because she had a high-risk pregnancy with twins and her still being sexually active with multiple sex partners.

Twan sat stuck with his jaw jacked wide open. He was shocked. Twins? And she'd already named them. This was too much for him all at once. What if they really were his twins, and she really did keep it 100% real with him? Now, she was useless to him, all fat and showing big time. Most tricks would see her profile online and then show up to the hotel, turning right around once they saw her huge stomach.

"Twan, I got the ultrasound pictures last week, and I want you to have them. Keep them in the frame. Now, baby, I hope I can come home soon, cuz you know how much I hate hotels. And you did me the same way my old dude did but worse! You ditched me for months now. Now, I can't turn a lot of tricks. So, what? You gonna put me out or send me back to New Orleans now? After I got you over a hundred racz, baby? Whatever, Twan, you know where I'll be at. You want ya first-born twins to be born in a funky hotel trick-turning room? Bye, Twan!" Diamond Cutz said in an exhausted tone as tears ran down both cheeks rapidly. Then she pulled out the ultrasound picture and told Twan to help her back down out his truck. Twan watched her wobble away and up the stairs. Then he saw Jill peeking out the hotel blinds and flicked her straight off.

He picked up the ultrasound pics and saw both heartbeats and his family nose and forehead outline, too. It hit him hard. These were his kids, and he was about to really be a daddy. He just needed a little more time and space from Diamond Cutz ass. He wasn't ready to be a father. He still had many years of big pimpin' ahead of him and to hit big like Barry Bonds. He just needed some real time to think about his next move. For once in his life, Twan wanted to ask Mama Lela for advice and what he should do. Then it hit him. He could have her stay in his old room at Mama Lela's crib. He vowed to come to get her next week. He texted her real quick and told her she could come home next week and finally get off her feet. She texted back, *Yeah, right!* And she'll believe it when she sees it. Twan didn't text her back and just left it alone.

That same day Diamond Cutz went over to Jill's room and asked her did she want anything from the store because she was going to buy some more condoms. She didn't want her babies to catch nothing she contracted from these pussy-paying tricks and dirty dicks. Jill told her she was all good and hated the Southside and being in this ratchett-ass hotel. She explained how cheap these niggas were and didn't want to pay for pussy, no more than a couple bucks to fuck. Then most dudes tried to rob her for the money or wanted to fuck first, then get up and leave without paying. Then Twan wanted to know why the tilt was short! He was never there for them, and Jill was sick of it and his shit.

Diamond Cutz wasn't trying to hear all of Jill's misery. She was struggling with her pregnancy. Diamond took her Gucci bag and hotel card and walked to the corner store. She wouldn't ask Jill for a ride anymore because she needed to walk and exercise. It was the doctor's orders. She would talk to the twins and tell them to stop fighting and Lil Twan to stop being bad. She felt them kicking all over her ribs and down on her uterus, too. She would put her Smartphone up to her stomach and play all her favorite iTunes ratchett songs and all. She stayed rubbing her belly. Every time she would turn a trick, and they'd hit it from the back, she would feel the left side always kicking. She knew it was little Twan, and he didn't like that shit. It seemed like he knew and hated what his Mama was doing. If an unborn child knew it was wrong and sensed bad vibes, then why Twan retarded ass couldn't wake up and see it, too? He needed to grow up!

She had a nice long walk to the store, getting some fresh air and sunlight. She enjoyed the Louisiana breeze. She went into the store and brought a box of Magnums and chocolate ice cream with some generic hot sauce. The store clerk just laughed at her. He was a cool square from Delaware. He didn't have sense enough to spit game or ask her how much to pay to play. She giggled at the nappy-head young un. The poor fella didn't have a blind shot in hell. She thanked him and told him to keep the change, too.

Twan was at home playing with Snack, trying to make him lock and shake like a pit bull. But his jaws weren't built like that. Snack was a French bulldog with a mean underbite. Miley was standing there with just her panties on with no bra when Twan's phone started going off back to back. Miley warned him to get his phone. It could be big business or an emergency. He told her they could text and quit blowing off his phone.

Finally, Twan told Miley to bring his phone. He checked the text from Jill saying 911 ASAP! She needed to holla at him about Diamond's ass. He just continued to ignore her texts and calls, thinking she and Diamond Cutz were arguing again. He texted Diamond and told her to cut all that bullshit out, and he was tired of their little drama over dominance. She didn't return his text. Jill stopped texting him after 1 a.m. He texted her once and told her, *Bitch, you better get back to work, hoe! Before I come down there and kick the shit out of ya ass again, hoe!*

The next day both his hoes at the hotel were quiet. He didn't receive a call or a single text. It was odd, but he liked it better that way. The next day went by, and he became curious, asking Miley had she heard from Jill or Diamond? She told him that Jill hadn't texted her in the past week, and Diamond hadn't called her in the past couple of days.

Then it hit him! She'd run away. *The bitch done went astray. Damn it!* He smashed a bit too hard on her. He told Miley to ride with him because he needed an extra set of hands. He floored the Escalade to the Southside while puffing on a blunt and taking swigs of the rest of the bumpy face gin he had left in his truck from the other day. All he thought was *how could Diamond smash out on him and run away with his twins?* He knew she probably ran with all his dough. She wasn't about to leave the stash and just say fuck him and go!

Twan pulled into the hotel parking lot, swaying the Escalade sideways on 6's, tearing his rims and tires up. Miley held on for dear life, thinking Twan was drunk out of his rabid-ass mind. Jill heard Twan's tires screeching, then a loud thud. She looked out the window and saw Twan trying to reverse out of the car he just smacked into. She shook her head and watched Twan jump out the truck, bubbly with an open bottle in his left hand. Miley was right behind him. He went to Diamond Cutz' room and banged and kicked the door, not giving a fuck about the manager calling the BRPD. Jill ran out there and told Twan to turn down a notch as she opened Diamond's room with the card.

Twan threw Jill out of the way and told her to shut up, bitch! Miley stood there, scared once again, as Twan rushed in and ransacked the room. He saw open old pizza boxes and all her clothes still there. Then he stuck his hand under the box spring and felt around until he found the stash. To his surprise, it was $460, all in twenties.

Twan was on his knees when he counted the dough. He left it on the floor and sat up on the bed. Miley and Jill were both looking down at the ground, dumbfounded. He looked at them, trying to see who knew what. He put his head up toward the ceiling. Something happened to the bitch, and Jill either did that something or didn't stop that something. She was responsible; she was the oldest. He rushed Jill and cold-cocked her right in her eye, instantly swelling it shut.

Jill threw her arms around her head and started screaming, "Help!" at the top of her lungs. Twan started kicking her rib cage in like a tire.

"Okay—T-T-Twan, I swear I don't know why she ran away or where to. I tried to tell you the first night! I swear—"

"Shut da fuck up, punk-ass bitch! You know that bitch missing and didn't run away! Unless she left all her shit here on purpose, money and all? Where she gonna go without dough? Huh?" *BAMM!* Twan yelled after he cut Jill off, and then kicked her again in her funky ass. That kick sparked an idea. Where was her phone? He told them to help him search the room for her phone. Diamond Cutz always kept two cell phones. Jill couldn't move. All she did was ball up on the floor in a fetal position as she held her fractured rib. It hurt her to breathe. She couldn't even get up if she wanted to. She thought Twan punctured her lung, too.

They searched the room hard, flipping over the bed and going in every crack in the walls until Twan got dizzy. He stopped and sighed out hard and deep. He was defeated and knew right then and there that Diamond Cutz ran away, despite how much he was in denial. The bitch was officially an astray hoe, and those never ever came back, not once. He would never see his twins. Probably when they got old enough, they'd come find him, but he'd be long gone out of BR, maybe in Hawaii or the West Indies somewhere. He heard police sirens and darted out the door, leaving Jill and Miley by themselves. It was save yourself time for Twan.

Twan stumbled down the steps, realizing Miley still had his truck keys. He shot out the back door like a track star. The sirens grew louder. He knew Jill was for sure likely to snitch on him after that ATL stomp-like beating. He also knew he couldn't go back to his house because it was in Jill's name, and she was sure to give them the address, too. The truck was in Jill's name, too. He was hit like good weed across the board. He ran down a few back streets, out of breath, holding his side in pain, trying to relieve his lungs and catch his breath. Then he pulled out his cell and searched for a number to a familiar person. He hated to do it but had to. He needed a ride to his Mama Lela's crib. He felt like he was back at square one, and things had gone from sugar to shit quick!

The BR police questioned Jill about what happened and asked who assaulted her. They had been called for a domestic violence dispute from different people in the hotel. There had been complaints of a woman screaming and crying for help. They took her with the ambulance to St. Joseph Hospital, then questioned Miley for the next 30 minutes. She, too, managed to keep her vow of silence, even though she was full of tears. Twan didn't know how lucky he was. These hoes weren't loyal, but these dudes were telling the feds on the street and in prison the whole rundown and names and numbers faster than these loose-lip hoes. They were no better.

Miley took off in Twan's Escalade. She sat bedside at Jill's hospital room. Jill convinced Miley to leave Twan because he was going to do her dirty and probably worse next and used Diamond Cutz as an example.

CHAPTER 10: N.O.

The Duplex and Club 360 was jumping in New Orleans. The whole mighty 9th Ward was across the river getting it in, ratchett hoes and all, big, small, fat, bald and all.

N.O. came back in town from BR that early morning and was already chasing tail and stunting, blowing big Kush blunts and sipping big bottles of rosé. He already felt rowdy. He was telling niggas and bitches he was 'bout it 'bout it whoadie!

He had come down to meet up with his Cuban connections. They had been doing biz for the last three years and would front N.O. as much weight as he could handle because they liked how he did biz and was about his paper and position to prosper up the drug chain. However, today was different. N.O. had been getting into it with the Cubans because the money was coming up short a few times. He didn't believe them at first, thinking they were always trying to get over on a nigga like he was dumb. Plus, they were being too greedy. He would always beg them to leave a little more meat on the bone, so he could really eat. The Cubans felt like N.O. was getting over, though, because the prices were more than right and far lower than the rest of the competition because they were the plug with the best uncut product. They had quality and knew N.O. could chop that shit up in four different ways. So, they weren't going. N.O. found out his little stripper bitch was peeling him and pinching his re-up stash. He knew that he was in violation of the ten crack commandments, and Biggie Smalls was right. He had let his guard down, got too comfortable, or pussy whipped. Instead of him killing the sneaky bitch, he had let it go.

Three weeks later she liq'd him for over a hundred racz and ran off with some pimp nigga in BR. He knew the bitch didn't go back home to N.O. She wasn't smart enough. She always needed attention and direction from someone. She wasn't dependent on herself. She was one of them bitches that couldn't be left alone. He shook his head and told the two hoes from uptown to come on. The trio left the joint and hopped in his Saints dunk on 30's skyscrapers all black and gold for that New Orleans color and crown. He felt he was king of the city because he was that dude. Really, he just ran the 9th Ward. Them niggas from 3rd Ward really ran Choppa-City. They named New Orleans Choppa-City from back in the days when they would hit the train stock cars for AK-47 assault rifles by the crates. For the next few years, New Orleans was the number one murder capital in the U.S., bypassing Cali. Everyone, from the little niggas to the old vet heads, were playing with them choppas. Fuck handguns giving a nigga the blues. Most of the city was dead and gone from that era. Now niggas were still getting their heads busted to the white meat, but it was this new generation skinny-jean-wearing snitch era. Half the city was Federal indicted, either in the county jail, or on the run O.T. somewhere. After Katrina, the city and the niggas have never been da same.

N.O. went back to the hotel to get his Nicki on with the two uptown hoes. They were doing tricks and acting a donkey as if he was 2Chainz. He enjoyed the freak show but couldn't get his mind off revenge. Pac said it was the sweetest joy next to getting pussy, too. He knew that sneaky hoe was still right there in BR. He had been trying to find her and that pimp nigga, too. Some people call him Slim; the others say his name was Twan. That sounded familiar, but he couldn't lace a face to the name. He did know a few Slims in BR and N.O., though.

The next morning at 9 a.m., he kicked the two uptown hoes out of his room and made them walk or catch a cab. He peeked out the blinds to check on his Saints dunk, making sure his wheels were all Gucci. He rolled up some dough and took a shot of the white. He scrolled through his phone with his right thumb and pressed the Cuban's number. He told him what hotel he was at and the suite number, too. He put the Gucci Mane song "Brickz" on his phone and laid it on the table as he dried the blunt with his Bic lighter, then sparked it and inhaled the purple smoke in his chest. He exhaled, coughing from his suffocated lungs. He looked up at the ceiling as he felt the Kush taking over his mind, body, and soul. He smirked, knowing he was blown.

N.O.'s face was tatted. He had 3 teardrops on his left side and 4 solid colored-in teardrops on his right side. He had a New Orleans Saints sign in the middle of his eyebrows and the letters N.O. tatted above his right eyebrow to the side like Tyga. He looked more like Mack Mane from Cash Money. He had a stocky build to him, even though he only stood 5'9". He was a fool and would kill at will. In the blink of an eye, you'd die. He kept a hair-trigger on the choppa and loved the sound of rapid gunfire. He loved to squeeze triggers and filing the firing pins down, too.

His body count was up there. He had smoked a few cats outside of clubs, in his hood, during licks, and at dice games, too. He never went to the County for one murder, because he went too hard. He warned any witnesses he'd hunt and kill a rat and chop-a-chop. He was a live fast, die faster ill nigga. Sometimes he would get wet off that New Orleans stanky sherm and leave a nigga stanky, leaking a bloody mess. After he got off stuck mode, he'd get so bombed out that he couldn't move, but once he came through, it was lights, camera, all action. N.O. felt like there were ten of him every time and was waiting for someone to say shit. He knew nobody couldn't fade this and start wetting whips up in traffic set tripping.

N.O. snapped out of his daze from the purple Kush as he heard his phone go off. It was the Cuban connection. He clutched his favorite German Uzi with a green laser beam on it. He was itching to eat a nigga face up with the hydro shock-tip 9mm bullets. Ewwhh…he could just imagine how their jaws would look a foot and a half away from their face. He tucked the Uzi behind his back after he kissed it. Then he went out to the parking lot of the hotel talking on the phone to the Cuban.

The Cuban pulled up with another car behind him with four Cubans in it. The first car there was four-deep, too. He didn't understand why they always came so damn deep everywhere. Like the plug was the Cuban president. All that shit made N.O. nervous every time. He warned Sosi's paranoid ass about how hot that was.

"¿Qué pasa, Sosi, mi amigo? I got $80,000 today 'cause I still don't got nobody I can trust with that much, especially after my lil mama got me. You was mad at me for weeks," N.O. said with a heavy NOLA gutter accent as the Cuban rolled down the window. Sosi told his ass to get in the front seat and kicked the passenger out, then took off with N.O.

N.O. sat uncomfortably, trying to not press his back too far on the seat while leaning on his left side. Sosi saw him squirming around uneasily and began to get nervous. Sosi's gunmen in the backseat saw Sosi's eyes light up.

B-BBBATTT! "AHWWHH shit, whoodie—FUCK!" N.O. yelled after his Uzi went off, eating up the front seat of the Dodge Magnum. *Click! Clack!* N.O. said what the fuck as the Cuban behind him put his right arm around his neck and Ruger up to his temple while the other Cuban in the backseat racked the Glock .45 to his side. N.O. asked Sosi to call his two goons off and that his Uzi just went off by accident as Sosi pulled the Magnum over. Now he was paranoid.

BAMM-BOPP! "Ugh…" N.O. grunted as the Cuban hit him twice with the butt of the Ruger, knocking N.O. into a weary state of unconsciousness. They rolled N.O. over and took his Uzi and dragged his body and stuffed him in the trunk of the Magnum, then drove off. Sosi knew he wasn't trying to jack him but he still didn't trust the black guys, and N.O. was the only one he ever did business with. Most of them didn't know how to keep doing good business. They'd get too greedy or too flashy, and flashy meant Feds or murder beefs from hungry wolves trying to take yours from every angle you didn't think of. Sosi scratched his balding head, then puffed on his Cuban cigar.

N.O. was awakened by Sosi. They let him out across the street from the hotel and gave his Uzi back without bullets, just in case he felt some type of way.

"Nothing personal, amigo," Sosi explained. "My men are cautious. That's why I take care of their families back in Cuba."

All the work was in the other car with the four Cubans that waited in the hotel parking lot. They got out and handed N.O. two duffle bags. One contained four pounds of raw, uncut heroin, and the other held three bricks of powder. Sosi always fronted N.O. because he always got the re-up and front money right back. This time he didn't bring much, and they still stuck him with a lot of work. He told Sosi to send someone up to BR to pick up the rest of the cash he had ready.

After Sosi pulled off, N.O. took the work into the hotel room. He scrolled through his iPhone and shook his head because he couldn't find a single hoe he could trust. Not even his sister or girl cousins. Then he checked his Uzi. Damn! Sosi had taken all his hydro shock tips out. He vowed to seek revenge and get some get back! Fuck them Cubans. They weren't about to pistol-whip him and play N.O. like a hoe. He wasn't going by far. He took a deep breath and said, "Fuck it!"

N.O. picked up the duffle bags and checked out the hotel room. He just had to have heart and drive the work to BR himself. He stopped by Walmart and bought some 9mm P.M.C. bullets for his Uzi. He was going to shoot it out with the Louisiana state troopers if they pulled his dunk over. He already made his mind up. It was catch me if you can like the gingerbread man. He plotted on his revenge against the Cubans the whole drive to BR.

Two weeks later, N.O. was still trapping tough. Both his business phones were going berserk off the hook when he got a call from Dreads. Dreads wanted to buy a quarter bird.

"Okay, $7,300. Dis shit fire," he said.

"Naw, man, $6,500. Remember when ya used to get 'em for $5,600?"

How times change with the border battle. "A'ight, fuck it. Come through ASAP with the whole $6,500, and I got chu."

"Hell yeah. Meet me at the 7-Eleven."

Dreads was from the projects around the corner by his B.M. house on the Southside and was doing big things for a project nigga. He would serve fiends and give double-ups to the homies and homegirls out there grinding hard.

Two hours later, N.O. and Dreads met at the 7Eleven. Dreads hopped into N.O.'s dunk, gave him some dap, and then threw him 6.5 racz.

N.O. sat there staring in a demonic daze, looking out his windshield. Dreads didn't know what was up. He looked around but didn't see anybody. He thought N.O. saw the BRPD or the Feds. N.O. had him super paranoid. He didn't even count the stacks like he usually did. They just sat in his lap still in rubber bands, all trap money.

"Yo, dog, you a'ight?"

"All Gucci, dog," N.O. said, still staring through the windshield. Then, he pulled out the nine-piece of soft from under his nuts and tossed it to Dreads. Then he tucked the $6,500 without looking at Dreads once. N.O. looked like he was stalking prey with the look of kill-kill on his face.

"A'ight, I'm out," Dreads said. "Hit chu later."

Dreads saw N.O. snatch his Uzi from under his front seat. Dreads quickly jumped out of the dunk. He didn't know what N.O.'s wild ass was up to or on, maybe a pill or something he was tripping on, but Dreads wasn't about to sit around and find out. He was a natural-born hustler, a straight D-boy. He hurried up and got in his B.M. car.

N.O. clutched his Uzi. Karma was a motherfucker! It was his bitch, Diamond Cutz. Did she really think she was going to liq him for over a hundred racz and get away with it? That killer instinct took over in him. He watched her pay for her stuff and wobble toward the front door. *Damn, she got fat as hell!* N.O. thought. Then he saw her big old stomach when she came out of the store. She was knotted up! He was about to really kill this bitch.

N.O. hopped out his dunk, running full speed ahead with his Uzi in hand. Diamond dropped her bags and tried her best to run as fast as she could. She had heard the bass thumping in the parking lot and had seen N.O.'s dunk. Fearing for her life, she ran around the corner of the store.

N.O. caught her by the dreads and busted her upside the head with the Uzi. Dreads just shook his head when he saw N.O. smack the pregnant bitch and drag her to his dunk, then throw her in as he pulled out of the parking lot.

N.O. was punching the dunk and pulled into the projects, which was a known high violent crime area. He dragged her out the dunk by her gold locks. She tried her best to kick and fight him back. N.O. cracked her jaw with one punch. She fell to the ground. N.O. pointed the Uzi toward her and let it erupt. Diamond's body jumped as three hollow tips tore through her small frame. N.O. took two steps and football punt-kicked her head. All that could be heard was a loud thud sound. Then, he spit on her as her body went limp.

"Stank bitch! Rot in peace! N.O. said. Then, he tucked the Uzi, hopped in his dunk, and smashed off.

A small crowd formed around Diamond Cutz' body, and someone phoned the ambulance. She was fucked up. They felt bad for the helpless pregnant girl. Her eyes were swollen shut, blood was leaking out her nose, and her jaw sat sideways. She had three oozing bullet holes in her stomach. They knew N.O. was ill to kill his own B.M. It took the ambulance almost 12 minutes to get there. They put an oxygen mask on her face, then pumped on her chest to get a heartbeat as they loaded her into the back of the ambulance. The ambulance drove off slow with no sirens on, which usually meant the person was dead or flatlined on the way to the hospital or a D.O.A. The crowd just all shook their heads as they watched the ambulance cruise away slowly.

Dreads got a text from his little homies saying that his dude was hot and making the bricks hot, too! Dreads knew exactly what and who his little homies were talking about. He usually stayed out of domestic disputes, especially anything unrelated to the projects, which was extremely rare because the projects were full of drama on top of drama.

N.O. was smashing the dunk, looking out his rearview mirror nervously as he wiped down the Uzi. He prayed he made it off the Southside safe. Now that he got some get-back on Diamond, it was time to get them damn Cubans. He called them to re-up and this time come to BR because he had a big spender.

CHAPTER 11: I'm Back

Neese picked up her phone after she got texted twice.

"Well, hello, stranger. Did you miss me, Pa? Huh? What's good? Are you ready to come home and be with ya wifey and leave them streets and ratchett-ass hoes alone?" Neese said in a sexy soft tone with her Creole accent.

Twan told Neese he wasn't trying to hear all that smoochy shit, and he needed her to pick him up and take him to Mama Lela's crib because he wrecked his truck and was more than likely on the run. Neese bought it and told Twan to stay on the phone with her while she drove to the Southside to pick his hot boy ass up. Twan knew he was about to hear an earful. He still wasn't about to take no hoe shit, but he knew after he dicked her down good and hard, just the way she loved it, that she would be Gucci.

Neese pulled back up, looking at a distressed Twan. She knew something else was bothering him. He was troubled, and it wasn't just a damn hit-and-run accident. He made her nervous, too. She was looking all around, asking Twan what happened and what did he really do? Twan told her he had to smash Jill ass out because she did something to his B.M. Diamond, or she more than likely knew what happened to her. Neese shook her head as she sucked her teeth, then called him a dummy. She told him he didn't care about that girl or them two damn kids because he wouldn't have had her out there on the stroll 6-7 months pregnant. Twan looked at her dumbfounded.

Then he got a text from Miley asking, *Daddy, where you at?* Twan really felt like she was setting him up with the BR police on the other end. He shut his phone off on the hoe, paranoid, thinking she was really trying to set him up and get his ass booked. Neese pulled up to Mama Lela's crib.

Twan slammed Neese's Impala door. "Stop always slamming my door, shit!"

Twan waved her off and went inside.

"Aww, my baby girl is back! Aww hell yeah, come give ya Mama Lela a hug, girl!" Mama Lela screamed.

"I'm back! And Twan ass ain't leaving my sight this time. He's done trying to be a pimp and messing with them nothing-ass ratchett hoes. Home is where the heart is…and he got all of this Creole loving, Mama Lela," Neese replied.

"Please, I'm keeping it pimpin' fa life, Neese! Y'all got a pimp fucked up. Just cuz I'm down on my luck don't mean shit! I can bounce back like crack!" Twan shouted, annoyed.

"Please, Neese, beat his ass for getting one of his little ratchett hoes pregnant instead of you," Mama Lela said.

Twan shook his head, got up, and walked to the room. Neese ran behind him and shook her head at Mama Lela. Mama Lela looked confused. She was lost and didn't know why Twan was acting so sensitive. Neese grabbed Twan, telling him to come here. Twan snatched his hand away and pushed her back. Neese shut his room door. Mama Lela grabbed her keys and her crackpipe. She was going over to Johnny Lee's house. She knew those two crazy-ass kids belonged together and were about to have some steaming make-up sex.

Neese rushed Twan, trying her best to wrestle with him until he slammed her on the bed. She bounced up and snatched Twan's pants by the waist, pulling him down on top of her. She held him and kissed him on his lips, passionately. Then she whispered in his ear she was sorry, and she needed him to fuck her good, and she wanted his baby, too. Twan's whole body just relaxed. He felt like taking some stress out. Plus, Neese's ass had gotten phat since the last time, and her hips and thighs had gotten thick.

Neese felt Twan stop resisting. She unbuckled his Gucci belt, unzipped his pants, and began slurping his knob like a vet. Neese straddled Twan and massaged her horny crevices slowly. Twan felt her wet warm vaginal canal. He tried to find a rubber quickly, but Neese locked his hand with hers. Twan said fuck it as Neese sat down on his throbbing dick. She rode him like a pony but in a passionate slow motion as Twan gripped her ass cheeks. Neese was kissing his neck, ears, and chest. She was making love to him for the first time. She was wetter than EVER! Twan loved every bit of her bumping and grinding slowly on his sword. They both climaxed at the same time and collapsed in ecstasy. They both lay there talking and cuddled up all night. Neese prayed Twan wouldn't leave her again and hoped she was back to stay this time.

The next evening Twan was trying to lay low, but Neese wanted to take him out to eat at the Southside Chicken Shack. Really, she just wanted to be seen and floss on them haters on FB and Twitter talking slick. She convinced Twan after rolling him some of that purple haze she got from one of her vics, always tricking for a licking or a sticking.

Twan tried to call Miley after he texted her twice. Her Twitter account was shut down, and her FB page had been deleted. He knew it was really a wrap, and Jill probably tricked Miley to leave a pimp, too. Fuck it: lose a hoe, gain two was the name of the game. It was all part of pimpin'. He didn't like no hot police-ass hoes. Once a bitch turned Feds, it was a wrap and no going back. With that thought, Twan chucked his phone out of Neese's passenger window.

Neese's eyes lit up! She was surprised and happy that everything went all wrong with his hoes because that meant she had him all to herself once again. "I'm back, bitches!" she mumbled to herself.

"What you say?" Twan asked, trying to figure out what she was babbling under her breath about.

Neese just shook her sneaky-ass head and said, "Nothing, Pa," as she smirked devilishly. Twan sat back and rubbed his head, listening to Drake sing "Started from the bottom, Now we here."

When Neese pulled her black Impala into the Chicken Shack, it was as packed as she'd expected. She and Twan got out and walked in. As soon as Twan went up to the counter, he was greeted by one of his pimp partners from Shreveport, LA, named Mac Petey. Mac Petey pulled Twan to the side and told him his little stripper hoe almost got fucked off and was in the hospital in bad shape. Twan was confused He asked Mac Petey which one? Mac Petey said the goldilocks hoe that used to dance at Lipstixx, and he knew for sure because his stripper hoe from the projects told him she was there when goldilocks got shot up. Twan was so shocked his jaw dropped. Neese was paying attention to her man, even though she was out of ear range. She was always trained to watch Twan's back. He wasn't the biggest nigga, and she had to help him a couple times before, especially with Big Brandon from high school, who would slam Twan around in front of everybody during school, at malls, or in the clubs. She shook her head. Twan just didn't have fighting bones in his body, unless he was cornered. It was instinct for her to watch over her Pa.

"So, let me get this shit straight, P… You say my hoe shot up in the hospital, and someone shot the bitch in the projects, right?" Twan asked in a stern tone, pissed off.

"Fa-sho, Pimpin'! And I know 'cause I used to jib at the lil bitch in Lipstixx when my project hoe used to dance up there. I used to sic my project bitch on dat hoe, but she wouldn't go! That's when a couple of weeks later, I heard you knocked the crazy lil New Orleans bitch!" Mac Petey replied as he notched his white Cuban brim.

"Digg dat, P… Aye, thanks fa the info, Mac Petey. Keep it pimpin'. I'll go check up on the hoe myself. I thought the hoe done went astray, but you know how this game goes. Cop and blow! We don't chase 'em. We replace 'em! Let me know if you find out who popped my lil New Orleans bitch, and I got cha, P–Chuchh!" Twan said in disbelief, trying to hide his pain as he gave Mac Petey the pimp shake. Mac Petey told him to be careful and keep his game tight. He smiled and pointed to Neese as he walked out, saying, "She a wild one."

Twan had lost his appetite, so he just watched Neese pig out. He needed a drink. He told Neese to take him to the hospital soon as they leave. Neese didn't understand, and Twan wouldn't budge. She kept asking him what was wrong and if he was Gucci. Twan wouldn't dare tell Neese what was really good. He knew she wouldn't drive him to the hospital and check on his shot up B.M. Twan had butterflies in his stomach. He feared the worst—that both his twin babies were hurt or gone. The suspense was a motherfucker.

Neese took Twan's food to go in a doggy bag. The whole ride to the hospital, Twan sat still and quiet. Neese rubbed on Twan's head like a baby. Twan was lost in deep thought. He never knew Diamond Cutz' real name, nor did he ever care about her gov either. Now he needed it. He decided to try to go room to room and fish a couple of nurses, saying he was looking for his pregnant sister that got shot carrying twins.

Neese followed behind Twan in the hospital, thinking he must be here to visit his bitch cousin Jill that he went ham on. She wasn't mad at him because she was still his cousin and family. She walked with him, confused as he went room to room, floor to floor, distressed. She couldn't understand why. If he knew Jill's name, what was the problem? Then she remembered he was on the run from the BR police, and usually, the detectives lurk around hospitals.

Finally, Twan reached the 5th floor, the maternity ward. He saw a fat nurse with light-green scrubs on and stopped her. He told her he was looking for his baby mama. She had been shot up in the projects while carrying his twins and she had gold dreads. The nurse shook her head and looked over at Neese, knowing it was Twan's main piece. Then she put her head down and pointed down the hall, telling him room 511.

All Neese saw was Twan talking to the nurse and then turn his head and dash up the hall. She tried to catch up with him, dropping her cell phone and keys. "Damn it, Twan!" she cursed.

Twan ran to room 511, took a deep breath, and pushed the door open slowly. Twan's eyes were shattered by first sight. He saw Diamond's deflated stomach and what looked like a million tubes running through her small arms. Her weary eyes got big as fisheyes. She started to shake her head as she tried to signal "No!" with her hand. Twan dropped a single tear and told Diamond he swore he was coming for her last week. Neese rushed into the door, seeing Diamond and instantly knowing she had been shot up a couple of times and lost the babies because she had bloodstained gauze on her stomach.

"Oh, hell nawh! Who dat? Is dat him, lil sis? Sabrina, this Twan ass, right? Oh yeah, nigga, you got to go, boy! I'm Sarah, Sabrina's older sister. Her jaw is wired shut and fractured in three different places, so she can't talk, and I'm talking for her. So, nigga, get the fuck out of this hospital room before I stab ya dumb ass myself. I'm serious, Twan, y'all don't got no more ties—her babies is gone. They both took a bullet apiece. The third bullet stuck too close to her spine and afraid she could go 6 feet under because it's by her heart, too. Now can you please leave? Now!" the gorgeous, super-thick redbone said as she stood all up in Twan's grill, clenching her fists.

Twan just stared at Diamond Cutz, devastated. Diamond had that look in her eyes like she still missed and loved Twan, but seeing him with that bitch Neese made her snap back to reality. She realized Twan didn't care for or love her and would never change his ways. She wanted to be out of the game, period, from strippin' to hoe'n. Neese just sat there, not daring to intervene. She knew Twan was dead wrong and wasn't shit, but that was her boo.

As soon as Diamond attempted to yell a muffled "Go!" through her wired jaws, Sarah lost it and went ape shit on Twan. She pushed him hard and started jigging him with her fingernail filer. Then Diamond hit her red help button. Neese got scared and backed up away from the crazy 30-year-old lady with the nail filer. Twan slipped in fear and fell on the ground. She quickly got on top of his head, stinging him like some bees with a five-piece combo. The acting nurse walked in and pulled Sarah off Twan, then yelled, "Security, room 511!"

Twan jumped up and ran over to Diamond and kissed her stomach and said, "Rest in peace, Lil Twan and my baby girl Twanita!" Then he grabbed Diamond's hand and told her he was sorry, and he wished he would've just left her alone at Lipstixx. Twan heard Neese say the security was coming down the hall, "Come on!"

Twan cocked back and pimp-slapped the shit out of Sarah, dropping her to the floor and leaving her screaming and holding her bloody lip. He darted out the door and down the hallway, trying to shake the off-duty cop. Neese ran the opposite direction as Twan crazy ass. She didn't know what Twan got her into, but she wasn't about to be his co-defendant and go back to the nasty BR County Jail again, especially in that black chair around all those stinking prostitutes. She would be there all day, relying on him to bail her out.

Twan hit the steps, trying to lose the out-of-shape off-duty cop, but he kept pursuing him. Twan was burnt out and had run all the way down to the basement floor with the morgue. He hid out for about 15 minutes with hopes of the cop thinking he fled out one of the working exits. He couldn't take that embalming fluid smell any longer and dashed for the exit. He finally saw Neese circling around the hospital in her Impala like a good bitch. He was glad she was back. He was about to go super hard and pimp harder on these hoes!

CHAPTER 12: Hitachi

Terrance, AKA TNut, was in his '79 blue box Chevy on 24-inch Lexanis. His B.G. Lil Uzi was riding shotgun with him as he pulled up to them niggas' hood under the bridge. TNut was meeting up with his dude that was more like family to him because they grew up together and went to the same schools since K-12. His best friend was Big Mikey. They called each other Bruh-Bruh. Mikey was from a Blood gang, and TNut was from a Crip set. However, TNut's hood was more about gangbanging, and Big Mikey's sett was about getting dough and stunting on them broke-ass hoods. So, TNut used to buy his dope from his dude Big Mikey. Big Mike lived right next door to Mama Lela for years.

Today Big Mikey was trapping too hard. He couldn't leave, so he told TNut to come through to the spot. TNut and Lil Uzi smoked on some sticky-icky and glided on 24's through the swamplands of BR. Lil Uzi had a Glock 17 ready. He was a young gunner and would smoke ya ass even though he was only 15 years old. He was TNut's brother Twan's age but a straight rider and had more heart than scary-ass Twan. TNut knew his bro Twan wasn't built like that. No matter how much he tried to make him a G, he just wasn't.

TNut and Lil Uzi pulled the blue Chevy up to the spot, beating Hurricane Chris's latest underground shit. TNut hit his horn twice. Big Mikey opened the door, flamed up in red-hot sauce colors, with his cell phone to his ear. He put his index finger up, signaling for TNut to hold on. Not even a full two minutes later, Big Mikey came out and sat in the backseat. He handed TNut four and a baby of hard. TNut threw him the dough and told Big Mikey Hell yeah and Teflon luv to him as they gave each other dap. As Big Mikey left the car, his cell went off again. He looked back at TNut and Lil Uzi and chucked up the deuce.

Once Big Mikey got back in his trap spot, he looked out the window and saw TNut get out and stash the dope by the battery in his hood. Then he saw his damn little homies pull up. It was Brazy Blood, Bam-Bam, and Lil CK. They all looked shermed out and burnt out, too. He knew they were coming to get a double up or a couple zips. *Damn!* Big Mikey thought, then hit Brazy Blood's phone, but he didn't answer. Big Mikey done told them little gangbanging niggas to get money and leave that bullshit alone, especially fucking with his family TNut. He had his whole hood believing he and TNut were real brothers. Today was different, and Big Mikey knew it. He opened the door and ran outside just as TNut was backing out and smashing off. Then Bam-Bam started tailing his bumper. "Fuck Blood!" Big Mikey yelled, thinking them little niggas better not bust on TNut.

TNut grabbed his .45 911 Colt. He told Lil Uzi to get his heat and be on point in case these little slob niggas tried to pull a stunt. Lil Uzi nodded his head up and down, clutching his Glock as he looked out his passenger mirror, peeping game. TNut was peeping game, too, through his rearview. He turned up his Hurricane Chris and let his 15's beat hard on them little niggas. He was halfway out of their hood when he saw the Tec-9 up out the passenger side window.

"Cuzz, get off! Lil Uzi, get him up off, you Crip!" TNut yelled as he steered with his left and pointed the .45 to the back window with his right hand.

Lil Uzi went to point his Glock out the window and turned his body around to bust, but he was too late. The Tec was getting off, eating up the blue Chevy box. Lil Uzi got off three shots before he caught a hot slug to the shoulder, which caused his Glock to drop into the backseat. He went to dive for it while the Tec slugs were still flying at the speed of light and caught him in the ankle, and he fell onto the backseat in pain.

TNut started letting the cannon go! He was just pointing and busting while trying to steer, getting low. He could barely see and was worried about Lil Uzi's young ass. He kept asking him if he was good. Lil Uzi couldn't find his Glock to get back off, especially how TNut was driving like a bad bat out of hell. The Tec-9 seemed like it would never stop running out of bullets! It felt like a lifetime as Lil Uzi's heart was beating hyper out of his chest for his life.

"Get them niggas, Blood!" Brazy Blood said as he rammed the back of TNut's box, trying to run him off the road before they made it all the way out of the hood. Lil CK put the Nina out the window and let it ring out. The fifth shot caught TNut in the back of his neck, causing him to swerve and crash into a parked car!

TNut just flew forward and broke his nose on the steering wheel, then he felt his neck leaking. As he tried to reach for his other clip through the broken glass on the floorboard, he got surrounded on both sides. He just closed his eyes and embraced his death, defeated…

"Blood, didn't I tell you niggas to stay out the hood? Fuck you and ya brotha Mikey, nigga! We run the hood, this redrum click, nigga—the lil homies is out cherr!" Brazy Blood screamed before he let his P89 go, releasing the whole clip while Lil CK whammied him from the other side. They hitachi'd TNut something crucial and left him stinking. Lil Uzi lay curled up under the backseat. He couldn't move because of his ankle. Big Mikey heard the shots ringing and that Tec-9 that Bam-Bam always carried! By the time he got to TNut, bullets had riddled the Chevy. It was too late. He peeked into the Chevy and saw TNut slumped sideways with holes all in his face and head. They made sure he was dead. He heard Lil Uzi moving around in the backseat, then the sirens coming.

"You hit? Come on! Let me get you to the hospital, dog!" Big Mikey said.

Lil Uzi said, "Nawh," still reaching for his Glock. There was no way Lil Uzi trusted Big Mikey. For all he knew, Mikey was the one to set his big homie TNut up.

Mikey saw the young un was leaking and paranoid. He let him be as he hopped in the smoker's bucket and punched out. Lil Uzi sat there with his deceased homie until the ambulance came. They took Lil Uzi to the hospital, and then cuffed him to the bed after a lot of questions and interviewing. For his non-cooperation, they charged his young ass with possession of a firearm and discharging a firearm in the Baton Rouge city limits. He was fucked and was charged as an adult.

* * *

Lil Uzi didn't get out until he was 19 years old. When he did, he got with his older cousin, Choppa Face, and smoked all three of the knuckleheads that popped him and murked his big homie TNut. It took him just two summers to track down and kill them one by one.

* * *

In 15 A.D., the ancient years of the samurai, they used swords instead of guns for weapons, like the famous Kensu or the ancient Japanese Hitachi. Hitachi was a top-of-the-line sword made with top-quality rare material that would cut straight through you. Some were double-edged like a cutlass sword. It would chop your head clean off. It was the ancient way of the samurai. A Choppa back then would've been a Hitachi sword, no doubt.

Everyone in Baton Rouge used the word Hitachi when someone got they wig split or cracked in some way or another, and even if you got struck in the dice game or laid down at court. Either way you got hitachi'd and hit in one way or another, just like Twan's older brother Terrance, a.k.a. TNut. Twan never had a vengeful bone in his body, even after seeing his older brother's closed casket and laying him to rest. After Lil Uzi got out the pen, he tried to get Twan to get some get-back on them Blood niggas who murked his big bro. Twan was out there calling himself pimpin'. Lil Uzi didn't understand because all he knew was go, plus Twan and TNut's daddy was a legend around BR. He had bodies and beat a couple of murder beefs. He had been one of the biggest smack and crack dealers in BR when Twan was young, and before Mama Lela started smoking crack. She used to hustle and would sell whole bricks. Now, she couldn't hold a whole slab, let alone a zip. She'd smoke it just as fast as she would get it. Twan was still Lil Uzi's dude. He had vowed to look after him because he felt guilty about TNut, and Twan was Lela's only son left. Maybe pimpin' was different and would keep him alive.

N.O. had taken pictures of 200 racz he had put up and been flipping. He told Sosi he had this nigga from Omaha, Nebraska, in town. He had been looking to do business with him and that he had Omaha and K.C., Missouri, on lock. The Omaha nigga had long cornrows with blue beads on the ends with a gold grill with 90 crushed diamonds. He was a corn-fed husky nigga with a gut named Big Fudd. Fudd was there to buy all the work that N.O. liq'd the Cubans for. He told N.O. he would cash him out for the lo-low, especially if N.O. was using him as part of his caper. N.O. told Fudd it wasn't about the dough. It was about some get-back and them funky-ass Cubans trying to play him like a hoe, not a nigga from the N.O.! He just couldn't go, especially now that he had a permanent knot in the back of his head.

He and Fudd kicked it at Lipstixx all Tuesday night. They had to meet Sosi and his crew that next afternoon. N.O. had made a vicious plan and worked on it for over a month now. He knew they always rolled two cars deep. The second car always had the work—mucho work! The first car had the Boss Man and the guns. He knew the Cubans were smart but not ambush smart, and their greed was their only downfall. He would Hitachi them with his foolproof plan.

He smirked as he hit the yac and gave Fudd's yellow ass some dap. He was about to spark them Cubans like the Fourth of July in New Orleans. He pulled back the top of his AR-15, cocking a round in the firing chamber. He had two 30-round drums on it. He called them nuts. They'd never make it back to Havana, Cuba, in one piece.

The Cubans pulled up to the Southside. They had only been in town for 15 minutes, they claimed, but N.O. knew better and that Sosi and his goons probably been in town for a day or two. Maybe since last night, but he wasn't no fool.

Sosi was looking nervous as he saw Fudd pull up in the out-of-town plates with N.O. in the backseat. It looked legitimate, though, like Big Fudd was there to cop some major work. The Cubans were all on point and kept a vigil. Sosi told N.O. to follow him to the Waffle House by the interstate. N.O. agreed but told Sosi his dude was willing to give up the 200 racz first to show good faith, and he wanted to meet him personally, so he could go down to New Orleans every couple weeks or so to cop his work. He was tired of being middleman by hustlers Hitachi'n him. Sosi shook his head and wanted to go to the Waffle House to sit down and see what type of vibe he got from this new Fudd guy. He was tired of N.O.'s cocky shit!

After a 40-minute sit-down with the duo, Sosi had a good vibe and agreed to go back to N.O.'s spot to run all the money through the money-counter machine. Back at the rental house with all stolen furniture that was a front, N.O. began to pass around shots of Patrón to everyone. The Cubans all accepted, including Sosi, for celebration, plus it helped calm his trigger-happy goons' jitter nerves down.

N.O. excused himself and went to the bathroom, where he strapped on the blue cop Kevlar vest. He pulled the AR-15 out of the bathtub shower curtains and ran out the bathroom like Tony Montana, guns blazing, but the AR-15 just clicked.

Sosi's eyes grew wide as he saw N.O. click the AR-15 at him. N.O. knew it was his firing pin from him always shaving it down. *Fuck!*

he thought as he racked the top of the AR-15 again and fired it at Sosi's head. The Cubans jumped up, and one shot hit Fudd in the chest while the other three returned fire at N.O.'s crazy ass. N.O. caught Sosi in the arm as he dove in the kitchen. The other Cubans followed suit, blazing their pistols! N.O. caught two of the Cubans in the upper torso with the AR-15. As he chased Sosi and his goons out the back door, he heard 4 to 5 loud shots and slid on the kitchen floor. He held his burning, oozing left ass cheek as he turned around and looked at Fudd.

"Damn, whoodie—you shot me, fool! You supposed to get them damn Cubans, not me, whoodie!" N.O. yelled in pain.

"Fuck you, nigga. You got me popped!" *DOOM-DOOM-DOOM!* Big Fudd screamed in pain, holding his wheezing chest, then let his .40 cal thump at N.O. again.

N.O. flinched as Fudd's unstable ass missed him with every bullet! Fudd blacked out while N.O. was trying to get his AR15 off the ground. He crawled to the living room and used the couch to pull himself up. He snatched the AR-15 and pointed it out the window as he caught the Cubans driving off. He let it rip, catching the first car but missing the second car with Sosi in it! Lucky bastard! The first car crashed into a house down the street. *Damn,* N.O. thought. Now he had to leave the work and cash right there. He even left his AR-15 as he limped out the back door. He cursed Fudd ass out, praying he was dead. If not, he was sure to kill him next. He called his nigga Dreads from the projects to come to pick him up.

* * *

Neese pulled back up to Mama Lela's crib. She patched Twan's dumb ass up from letting Diamond's older sister dig him out with a simple fingernail filer. Twan wouldn't talk much. For two weeks, he stayed in the house, depressed, talking about he was just thinking of a master plan to bounce back. He stayed online looking for hoes, doing all that slick texting and shooting slick messages to hoes across the map. Neese thought when he lost his twins, he lost his damn mind. She was already tired of cooking and cleaning for his lazy ass. Maybe it would've been different if she was getting some good dick, but he wasn't even fucking her. When they did fuck, he'd lazy fuck her and then pull out. She wanted a baby. She was plain sick of his ass. When they started fighting, Neese got fed up and went to her mama's house for a couple of days, but she couldn't stay away from Twan's dumb ass for too long. By the time she came back around, Twan was back on his feet, talking about he knocked two hoes from Virginia and West Baltimore. He told Neese that was long-range pimpin', called L.R.P.'s, and his hoes were both on their way to BR on a Greyhound and would be there within the next few days.

Neese instantly fell into a shitty mood. Now it was her turn to act retarded. She dreaded what was to come next—Twan ditching her ass once again. She was tired of being temporary. She wasn't a temporary hoe by far.

Twan told Neese not to trip. She was going to be his bottom bitch for life.

"Get dressed. We goin' out to celebrate and congratulate, not hate. Put on yo best hoe outfit, so we can step out right," Twan said.

Neese backed out of Mama Lela's driveway with a stinking-ass attitude. Twan kissed her on her cheek and told her she still was his number-one stunter, that she just needed to stop being lazy and sell some of that sweet pussy for him.

"Uhh-no! Twan, been there, done dat for your stupid ass, but it still wasn't good enough for you, boy! Twan, it's been six whole long years that I've been here for you. I even disrespected my own Mom for your dumb stupid-ass sex games, boy! I did everything under the sun for your ass, Twan…but you still treat me like shit and continue to drag me through the mud in front of BR and treat me like shit, but somehow, I'm still here? I'm the dumb one! They say insane is when you keep doing the same things that you know is wrong or bad for you over and over again!" Neese whimpered as she wiped the streaming tears from her eyes.

"Neese, bitch, stop crying. We about to go to the House of Blues so the whole BR can see us so fly and high together! They all know I love your ass, and you forever, my bottom bitch. Let's forget about the past and celebrate for another six years strong together! Who knows? When I'm done with this pimpin' shit—I'll probably end up marrying you. You're my vet hoe! Neese. You know I love ya sexy Creole ass. You my Beyoncé, baby! Mmwwahh…" Twan blew Neese's head up with hot air bullshit.

Neese knew Twan was talking out the side of his neck like the Ying-Yang Twins, but she needed it. She needed to hear those words, the right words, and long-term insurance because she truly loved Twan and all his ways, even when he gamed her ass. She wiped her eyes and nose, then told Twan to shut up. He didn't love her and told him we'll see if she had a ring in another six years. If not, she was going to remind him of this very day. She'll never forget.

* * *

"Hitachi! Hitachi! Hitachi-Hitachi-Hitachi! Medusa head on me like I'm Illuminati," N.O. spit the Migos from Atlanta "Versace" song remixed in his own Hitachi version because that was how he felt. He had caught one in his ass from his own partner and missed Sosi altogether. His plan had backfired. It literally came back to pop him on his ass. He had been out of the hospital for two weeks now. He suffered a 200-rac loss terribly. He was trying to bounce back with the little bit of dope he had left, like a half of brick and a quarter pound of heroin. He wasn't at the bottom of the barrel, but he surely felt like it without his Cuban plug. He could see it.

Now he had the Cubans looking for him, probably hunting for him like some wild game in the swampy marshlands. He wasn't tripping or running. He didn't believe in hiding, just riding to the fullest. He was out, chherr! He had his German Choppa on his lap with a 50-round drum. It had the folding stock that he screwed off and just held the pistol-grip wooden handle. It looked more vicious and greedier. His Clarion shuffled to that Plies song, "My goons will bring me Bin Laden…" He nodded his head to the killer beat as he hit the danky weed, sucking on his gold slugs on high alert.

He stopped for a red light on the Southside and noticed a familiar black Impala, then when the light turned green, he saw a redbone driving on 22-inch chrome rims. Then it hit him. He said, "Ahh yeah!" as he flipped a bitch, then said, "Hitachi-Hitachi-Hitachiii!" animated as he cut the four 15's up and hit the yac hard again. He was in love with his sweet bitch named Karma, especially how she squirted every time she came.

Twan heard somebody shit beating out of control. It was hitting over Neese's little raggedy-ass 12-inch kickers. And she had a 1000-watt competition amp, too. Neese started looking in her rearview and side mirrors, then she turned around a few times. Twan never saw her so disturbed. He sat up and looked in his passenger-side mirror and just saw lights. Then he turned around and saw a black dunk. He leaned right back, slouched down far back, reclining behind tint, getting bent before they went into the House of Blues. Twan said, "Why you so damn jittery and nervous for?"

Neese was quiet for a few seconds, then she cracked open her mouth, "Ummh…shit…Pa, remember when you got out the County the last time, and you had me call my Mom to tell her I love ya crazy ass? Well, then you had me call a few niggas I had been fucking and tell them you was home now, and I'm charging them now to play, right? Well, the nigga that I called when I was giving you head and sent them selfies to after you skeeted all over my face—"

"Yeah? Get to the point, Neese! So, what?" Twan said, bubbly, cutting her off.

"Well—Daddy, that's who is behind us. That crazy nigga named N.O. Remember, Twan?" Neese said. Twan could hear the fear in her voice.

"And…so what? Fuck N.O. with his bitch ass! I don't care. Now stop acting scary, bitch!" Twan replied, annoyed, as he looked back in the mirror watching N.O. make his dunk dance as he swerved to the beat like a madman.

"Pssh…Twan, remember he threatened me and put that on his hood when I saw him, I better duck 'cause he gonna bust!" Neese said nervously, which now had Twan paranoid. He looked at Neese bug-eyed and told her to turn off and go.

As soon as Neese attempted to turn off, N.O. rammed her Impala. His bumper hit her trunk. Neese fishtailed and almost lost control! She started screaming. Twan told her to shut up and smash off. She put her foot all the way down on the gas pedal as the Impala's horses started moving. She blew through two stop signs and was coming up on a busy main street. She slowed down. Twan told her to go. Then he pressed her right knee down causing her to floor the accelerator. She screamed at Twan and told him No!

BOOM—SMACK! Errree… The Impala got T-boned by a white four-door Pontiac that had a family of three in it. The passenger flew through the windshield a couple feet, instantly killing her, snapping her brain stem tragically. The scene was a bloody mess. Twan was in a daze. He had it the worst and got T boned on his side. Neese had a cut-up face and glass in her hair. She suffered a terrible whiplash, too.

Twan could hear the dunk approaching in the distance, growing louder and nearer. He could barely move. Neese could hear him mumbling. She was in shock but said, "Twan, don't move, baby."

RRR—Rhddatt! R-Rhddatt! R-R-RRhddatt! Rh-Rh-Rhddat! N.O. saw she wrecked trying to get away from him, then pulled the dunk sideways and got halfway out the window with the Choppa-47 and let it *churrp-churrp* as it rocked the 2009 Impala. He left it looking like Iraq after they found Saddam Hussein's ass. He heard the horn blaring. That's how he knew he caught the stinking bitch and left her stinking for real! He didn't discriminate. He done murdered two hoes now in less than two months. Maggot-ass hoes will get you killed or an L!

CHAPTER 13: Revenge

Twan woke up in the hospital in pain. He had suffered three broken ribs and a severe concussion. He faded in and out of consciousness. Mama Lela was right there at his bedside. She hadn't slept or smoked any crack in two whole days! She didn't care. She was worried about Twan's life. She didn't understand what he and Neese had done.

"M-Mama, where Neese at? Mah-Mama…" Twan struggled to say.

"Shh…Shh…Twan, just relax, baby. Neese alright. Trust me, she in a better place, son. Now who did this to y'all?" Mama Lela said in a mothering tone.

Then Twan started having flashbacks from the other night. It all seemed like a nightmare that kept replaying in his head. The morphine in his I.V. didn't help. It seemed like it enhanced his vivid mental stage of awareness. Those Choppa rocks tore through the whip. Neese got struck multiple times. It looked like her whole body split in half. Her entire torso was in her lap as her head slumped on the lower part of the steering wheel. She died looking at Twan with her light-brown eyes open with her hand on his leg. The first bullet that hit her knocked her breath right out of her viciously. It had sounded like one big brief hiccup. He saw her lower intestine flopping out. She was gone before the rest of the AK-47 bullets tore her apart!

Tears trickled down Twan's cheeks. He couldn't believe he didn't get hit and hated Neese got the short end of the stick. He blamed himself. It was all his fault. Then he remembered what Neese said: "N.O." He then remembered today he was supposed to pick up his new fresh merch from Baltimore and Virginia, too. He vowed for vengeance! He would get revenge this time.

He didn't tell the homicide detectives shit, and no witnesses came forward. The BR detectives didn't know what the hell happened. All they knew was they had two dead bodies because Twan and Neese were running from someone. After they concluded their investigation and interrogation on Twan, they left his hospital room. Twan was happy he was in the clear. Nowadays, they had that dumb-ass felony murder rule catch-22. Long as they could place you in a commission of a felony and a body fell from either party, you were bammed, no questions asked. Twan wouldn't have seen daylight or stood a chance at trial. He never told them or Mama Lela anything, just that he didn't know what happened because he was too drunk and couldn't remember. He wouldn't dare to say N.O.'s handle because he wanted him personally.

Mama Lela knew Twan played on the fact they found blood alcohol in his system twice the legal limit and knew he was impaired, but Mama Lela wasn't a fool. She knew better. She didn't buy that dumb alibi shit he told them crackers. She was from the hood and street-raised. She saw that murder-murder-murder and kill-kill-kill look all over Twan's face. It was the same look that his older brother Terrance, a.k.a. TNut, used to have after their daddy got 25 to life in Angola State Prison. She just prayed Twan was careful and was smart about it. She knew he wasn't a killer, but someone had pushed her baby and killing was in his blood. His switch just had to be cut on, but she was afraid it wouldn't go back off that easy once young Twan got a taste of blood on his little growling fangs. Mama Lela told Twan she loved him and to be careful because she didn't want to lose her only son to the streets. She left the hospital room in tears. Right then, she knew she had to stop smoking and get cleaned up.

Twan was released from the hospital three days later, just in time to attend Neese's funeral. He had missed the open-door wake. Mama Lela showed up on Twan's behalf and to pay her own respects. Twan was doped up off Vicodin pain pills, and he had been smoking and drinking. He wasn't quite ready to see Neese like that. He had cold chills as if she could yell at him from her casket. She would tell Twan, "Now see what you did? You got me killed, dummy!"

Twan tried to shake off those thoughts. He wheeled himself into the packed funeral parlor. Attendance was high. Neese's family from Shreveport, Lake Charles, Monroe, and New Orleans came. Twan had never seen so many damn Creoles in his life. It seemed like half of BR was in there and all her high school BFFs, too. It was standing room only. Twan saw a few of his day-one homies from back in the days, too. Neese's Mom was up front, sprawled out over Neese's casket crying hard in a slumber of madness. She hated Twan for her daughter's death. She didn't care if Twan was all banged up. He wasn't shot all up or dead like her daughter was. Twan kept his distance but stayed for the full service. He had to see his best loyal hoe off and in style like a boss bitch that she was. When it was time for everyone to pay their respects and say their final goodbyes, they lined up to file past the casket one by one. Twan rolled past Neese's Mom and apologized, giving his deepest sympathy. It fell on deaf ears; Neese's mom was numb to everything. She had been through too much pain since she got that heart-dropping, gut-wrenching call about her daughter's death.

Then, it was Twan's turn. He pulled up on Neese and put the flowers in her casket. Then he stood up out of the wheelchair and leaned on his good left leg. He saw Neese's stiff body with her hands straight down to her sides tucked in tightly. She rested in a cream-colored casket. She was appeared to be sleeping. Her red dress fit her perfectly, and she looked like a stunting Barbie doll. Her make-up almost matched her real skin tone; it was a few shades darker, but you could tell it was Neese. Her hair was done up nicely, but it was clear to Twan that they could've put more time into it. Twan felt angry because he couldn't even contribute. He was right back at the bottom for real, not just of the map but the bucket.

Twan lost it when he kissed Neese on her glued cold lips. The whole funeral home lost it, and everyone started pouring down crying once Twan broke down bawling. He was whimpering like a puppy dog, dangling off the front of her casket, saying how sorry he was as if she could still hear him. Twan was holding up the funeral, and a few people left in the viewing line.

Lil Uzi, one of his brother's childhood little friends, came to help Twan pull himself together. Twan grabbed Lil Uzi and told him they killed his bitch! Lil Uzi told him he knew and had his back fade as he embraced Twan with a thug hug. Twan hugged him back and told Lil Uzi, "Yeah, some get-back... It was a nigga in a dunk named N.O. I'm ready, Uzi. Let's roll. I'm ready to ride out, cuz... Let's stink that nigga!" Twan mumbled, trying to whisper in Lil Uzi's ear.

Mama Lela sat in the back of the funeral in her best put-together outfit. She hadn't been out in years since she'd started smoking heavy dope. She saw Twan with that kill-murder blood face and knew T-Nut's little homie and he were plotting revenge, bloody revenge. She just wanted Twan to be on point and hoped he got away with it.

After they laid Neese to rest in Baton Rouge's oldest cemetery, it was on. Twan's eyes were bloodshot. He was drained out. If he had any chance at love or to be in love with any hoe, it would've been Neese. Now he really was a pimp for life.

There was a blood moon that night. They say it's when the dust and rays are reflected off the earth by the sun. It makes the moon look red. Twan felt like he was living in the last book of Revelation in straight hell where it's kill or be killed.

Lil Uzi passed him the bumpy face gin. They had been together all day since the funeral. Twan hadn't seen Lil Uzi in years, probably since they were both in the BR County Jail together. Lil Uzi had put some size on him and had grown a few more inches. He was tatted up and forever trill. He told Twan that Lil Boosie just got free, and everyone was going down to his and Weebie's studio where they had all their colored Challengers and Chargers. TNut used to go to school with Lil Boosie and knew him personally. He was a real Boosie fan because that was his dude.

A white '79 2-door Chevy Malibu pulled up, beating hard, at the spot. It was Lil Uzi's big cuzzo, Choppa Face. Choppa Face was an O.G. from the hood. He had a picture of an actual AK-47 tatted on his face that made him look super ill. He had a Crip hand sign tatted on his other left side, too. He was a light-skinned, tatted-up nigga with a 5'10" stocky frame. Choppa Face got out and left his Bu running letting his music beat. He was out here on 30 Locs as he called it. Choppa Face been riding high since he was young. He walked up and did the hood handshake with Lil Uzi, and then gave Twan some daps.

"Twan Locsta, what's Gucci with you, lil cuzzo? I haven't seen you in the hood since ya bro TNut got smoked. You don't look too good pimpin', by far! Lil Uzi told me ya ol girl Neese got murked and chopped all up! You know I'm with the biz. I do this shit fa real. Just point, my nucca!" Choppa Face said without moving a muscle on his face.

He looked over at Lil Uzi for approval. Lil Uzi nodded his head, then shrugged his shoulders like he didn't give a fuck. Twan noticed that Lil Uzi had an actual Uzi tatted on his right cheek, too. He didn't know what was up with all the homies nowadays tatting their faces up. They were all trying to be like Choppa Face with his 12 face tatts. Choppa Face was a true diehard hood nigga, period, and down for life. He had done ten flat years in prison. He didn't give a fuck about the world or a damn job. Fuck slaving for the white man! He was going to get it how he lived. Choppa Face was the type of nigga that treated everyone like they were telling and were all suspect. If he didn't know you, he wasn't messing with you; and if he did know you, he still wasn't messing with you! He was just one of them type niggas.

Twan told him it's some nigga named N.O. who drives a Saints dunk. Choppa Face already knew precisely who Twan was referring to. He knew exactly who to call, Dreads from the projects. He knew that was Dreads' dude who he would cop some zips from. Choppa Face used to beg Dreads to let him liq his plug and say fuck that out-of-town ass nigga! Dreads wasn't going. He was no fool and would always tell Choppa Face he wasn't supposed to rob a good plug, and that's what was the matter with all the homies now. He didn't care if Choppa Face used to fuck with his ratchett black ass sister with her blue weave.

Choppa Face texted Dreads and told him to pull up to the hood to chop-it-up ASAP. He put 911. They sat there and drank, listening to Choppa Face's trunk rattle.

All Twan could do was think about Neese. He just couldn't get her out of his head. It was hard to find a hoe nowadays that'd literally die for you, especially for Twan's ratchett ass. He used to talk so sweet to Neese and game her so damn tough with his two slick peeling gold fangs. He talked so slick he used to have Neese sucking his dick like he was a million-dollar ass nigga or like he was a pretty boy that demanded top-notch hoes only. That's probably why N.O. tricked her out of her panties because she was so damn easy to game. All you had to do was pump her head straight up. It never failed Twan.

Then it made him think about N.O. again. All he saw was blood in his eyes. It was Hitachi season! Twan said, "Hitachi," animated.

Dreads hit Choppa Face back and told him to meet him at the Loves outside his hood. Dreads was a Blood, and his hood always had rival beef with Choppa Face's hood. They had been killing each other since day one, way before they smoked TNut. Baton Rouge was just so damn small that everybody's hoods bought dope from each other, the Crips, Bloods, and the Gangsters. Dreads and Choppa Face were both some O.G.'s and both did time in the joint together, so they could see past all the bullshit.

Choppa Face met up with Dreads and told him all the gruesome details and how that nigga N.O. had to go. He told Dreads he would owe him one if he'd help set up the play for N.O. so Choppa Face could leave him stinky. Dreads knew Choppa Face was serious and what this could mean. His greed got the best of him. He kindly accepted, letting Choppa Face know he indeed owed him a big one. He had ulterior motives to knock off one of his most fierce competition, J-Money ass. He would clock major dollars with J-Money's ass spread all around the swamp, eaten by them gators. He told Choppa Face to give him two days to set up the play. Then he told him how N.O. also shot up a pregnant girl in his hood, making them look like they did it, and blowing up the spot and making the whole projects on smoking 400-degree fire. Choppa Face told Dreads to keep the rest of the blunt of sticky they were puffing on, then gave Dreads some dap and smashed back to the hood in his Malibu. When he went back, Lil Uzi and Twan were gone. They said Twan was too scummy drunk and crying over Neese, throwing up. He was too feeble.

* * *

N.O. had been in a Budget car rental. His Saints dunk was too hot with the law. He was ready to take three or four of them pigs down with him. He would forever hold court in the streets. He was street born, street bred, and knew he would be street dead. It was just the rules he lived by. Never let anyone play you like a hoe. He rubbed his baby Choppa-47 on his lap as he hit the swisher sweet blunt. It was the same dirty Choppa that killed Neese. He didn't give a fuck if it was dirty or had a body on it. Most choppas did in the hood anyway. They were all throwaways and were guns made specifically for Hitachi season.

He met up with Dreads. They drove around in the rental chop-n-it up and networking, smoking sour diesel Dreads had gotten from his Colorado Springs plug. Everything was Gucci. N.O. felt Dreads trying to get really on now.

* * *

Mama Lela rocked back and forth, trying to shake the crack straight off cold turkey as she watched over a banged-up Twan in a drunken slumber. Her whole body going through it. Her mouth and lips kept getting dry. She was struggling; the crack cravings were too much for her. She continued to rock herself until the sun came back up. She felt like shit and hadn't slept in almost 72 hours. She was too worried about Twan and praying she didn't lose him.

"Twan, baby, wake up! Here, I made you some soup and fixed you some hot bathwater, so you can soak them sore bones. C'mon, eat this and get up—Here!" Mama Lela said as she attempted to spoon-feed Twan.

Twan wiped his eyes and took the bowl of Campbell's soup that Mama Lela made him. He noticed her dark circles were starting to clear up, too. After he ate the soup, he limped down the hall to the bathroom and slid into the tub. An hour and a half later, Mama Lela bust through the bathroom door and woke Twan up. She knew he was asleep. She was afraid he would doze off and slip under the water. Twan told her he was getting out, then fell right back to sleep in the tub. The second time she came and let out the dirty tub water. Twan left two rings around the tub full of a lot of dirt and alcohol.

Twan told her to grab her phone. He texted Lil Uzi to see what was the latest and greatest. Lil Uzi told him it'll be a couple more days and for him to just lean back and relax. Twan couldn't just relax. He was in pain, both physically and mentally. He needed a heater fast. He wanted to go out and hunt for N.O. himself. He asked Mama Lela, can he use her rusted old .38 that his daddy gave her? She would never sell it because it was the only thing she had left that he gave her besides Twan. She had smoked up everything else, from the furniture set down to the spoons.

Mama Lela drove Twan to the Waffle House since he was restless. She had Johnny Lee's truck. She helped Twan out of the truck, and they sat at a table toward the back. As soon as Twan sat down, he saw Mac Petey. Mac Petey barely recognized Twan without his strings on. Twan looked like shit like he had been dragged through the worst pits of hell for a day. Mac Petey called a limping Twan to his table and greeted him in pimp language.

Twan sat down right across from one of Mac Petey's hoes, and the other one was right next to him. One of the hoes smelled like she'd been at the truck stop and working bars judging from the odor of stale cigarettes and diesel fuel. The other had a stank clammy smell like she had an STD. Mac Petey didn't give a fuck what them hoes had, long as they kept getting his dough. He was a different pimp than Twan. He didn't believe in getting them hoes their shots and check-ups. He didn't believe in lecturing his hoes on self-preservation do's and don'ts. They chopped it up for a hot minute. Then when Twan told him what happened to him and Neese, it hit Mac Petey.

"Awwh yeah…P, I found out who wet up ya lil stripper hoe in them bricks. It was some nigga named—N.O.! He drove a black-and-gold New Orleans Saints dunk on black-and-gold 6's or 8's? You probably seen that nigga around the South selling dope? He a trigger-happy D-Boy," Mac Petey broke the news to Twan nonchalantly.

"Whattt?" Twan yelled as he pounded the table and stood up, scaring Mac Petey's two hoes. "Fuck—that's the same nigga who chopped us up, too. He Hitachi'd Neese and my twins. I do remember seeing that same black dunk at Lipstixx! Hell nawh, he killed my twins. It's a wrap, jack. I'm a get him. He forcing my hand and trying to test a pimp! Real shit! P, you know I appreciate the FYI—Keep smashin' on hoes. I'm gone!" Twan said.

Mac Petey replied, "Aiight, Twan. Go get his muthafuckin' ass!"

Twan told Mama Lela to drop him off in the hood. He called Lil Uzi straight up and told him to wake up because he was on his way over to his crib. Twan threw Mama Lela her phone back, then popped three perk 30's to ease the pain.

Three days later, N.O. was on his way to Dreads' B.M. house to sell him nine ounces of powder. Dreads was stepping his game up lately. He was a natural-born hustler. Dreads let N.O. come in the crib right as his B.M. was leaving. The plan was for him to get the nine zips first. He left the back door open. Lil Uzi was the first one in, then Choppa Face with a limping Twan. They all were strapped up. Twan carried the old rusted .38. He had six shots with N.O.'s name all on it. Dreads heard his B.M.'s wooden floor creak a little. He switched subjects on N.O., then asked him why he didn't murk Neese's dude, the pimp nigga named Twan. A big light went off in his head. The name Twan? And him being a pimp, too. That's where he heard Twan, the pimp that took his hoe Diamond and turned her out, turning tricks all over BR. He probably pumped the bitch up to hit N.O.'s stash for over 100 racz, too. N.O. scratched his head and then stood up.

"So, do you know who this Twan character is? Or where he at? I'll throw you another nine zips on the strength if you lead me to him, Dreads. Don't trip. I got cha, my dude, fa-real!" N.O. said with vengeance on his tongue, looking Dreads square in his eyes.

Lil Uzi popped out the kitchen with two twin Glock 40s. Choppa Face was right behind him with an SKS assault rifle. Twan stayed behind just in case they didn't successfully secure the living room area. Dreads' eyes lit up! He couldn't believe Choppa Face had brought Lil Uzi with him. He knew their history and that Lil Uzi knocked off three homies from his hood and killed his relative, little Bam-Bam. Then he started getting paranoid, thinking Choppa Face backdoored him for Lil Uzi to stink him, too. He looked over at N.O., stuck playing with the dope. N.O. felt set up flat out. He still wasn't going, though. Lil Uzi told them to put their hands up high. Dreads was the first one to buck. He quickly drew back down on Lil Uzi.

Bloch! Bloch! Bloch! —DOOM-DOOM-DOOM-DOOM! *FFhhdatt! F-F-Fhhdatt! DOO-DOO-DOO-DOO! POP!* Different gunfire exchange rang out like some loud cannons going off in the house living quarters. And bodies dropping.

Dreads got off first at Lil Uzi's torso. Lil Uzi got back off at Dreads, missing him. Choppa Face made the SKS spark, killing Dreads while standing. Then N.O. got off with his Mac 10, dropping Choppa Face to the ground. Twan let off one single shot with the old rusty trusty .38. He caught N.O. in the rib, which broke it and punctured his left lung. Then it came out of his neck upwards. N.O. dropped and spasmed for air with his collapsed lung. Twan limped up to N.O. and spit on him.

"Ain't no fun when the pimp got the gun! I'm a make you suffer. I'll punish ya ass. Nigga, you like killing hoes and kids, huh?" *Pow-Pow!* Twan said with an awkward face of revenge, then shot N.O. in his stomach twice. N.O. grunted and held his stomach as he was choking on his own blood in shock. N.O. raised his middle finger toward Twan. Twan smirked a devilish grin, and the last thing N.O. ever saw was a black barrel between his eyes. Twan pulled the trigger slowly, with a soft touch. It just felt sweeter.

He sat there for a second to get a good picture of N.O.'s disfigured dead face, so every time he thought of Neese or his twins, he'd also see how sweet the bitch revenge was to him. He wiped the blood spurts off his hand and sleeves. He tucked the old .38 in his waist and limped through the back way. He left Choppa Face's dunk there and called Mama Lela to pick him up from the Walgreens, so he could be inside away from the law.

Mama Lela saw Twan and knew he had done it. His daddy and his brother Terrance had the same killer look. Once they got back at the crib, she told Twan to wash his whole arms and face down with Pine-Sol to kill the gunpowder residue. She took her old rusty .38 and buried it in the backyard. Twan wondered why it was always rusty.

Maybe because it had been buried before and already had a body on it?

Twan washed up and smoked a blunt to calm his dancing nerves. He thought about the crazy change of events within this last year. He hated it and knew he had to get out of Baton Rouge. He knew that the Baton Rouge detectives would come to question him because the streets always talked, or one of N.O.'s goons would drive up from 9th Ward and murk him. He was officially a hot boy and on the run. He had lost a crib, a truck, his whole stable, and the hundred racz!

He gathered a few outfits he had and the dub sack of weed and got dressed. He told Mama Lela to spot him a few dollars and drop him off at the Greyhound bus station. She told him she's not about to lose him, and that she was coming with him. She told him she was done smoking crack and would go to rehab. Besides, she was his Mama. She was going to take care of him. Twan told her he would go to any mall and start off and knock a fresh hoe. She asked Twan, where was he going? He said he had the dirty South in mind. She told him the pimps had the South too hot for setting hoes down. The Feds were sweeping up pimps for white slavery, taking hoes across state lines, and that carried a life sentence. She told him more like the West Coast because they had a lot going on with more people. It wasn't just pimpin' as a hustle, so the Feds had more things to target. Then she told Twan she could be his hoe and pull herself together. She would bring him young hoes and train them right.

Twan thought about it. She did know the ropes, and he already had pimped on his cousin. Mama Lela still had a booty. *This just might work*, Twan thought.

"Sunset Blvd. in Cali," Twan said.

Mama Lela replied, "Nawh, Vegas, baby."

Twan yelled, "Vegas, here Pimpin' come!"

EPILOGUE

Twan and Mama Lela purchased one-way tickets to Las Vegas at the downtown Baton Rouge bus terminal. They were headed for new beginnings, a breath of fresh air. Twan had been nervous. They both were leaving skeletons behind in BR. All Twan knew was the Southside. The whole bus ride, he couldn't sleep. They drove through Texas, New Mexico, and Arizona. He saw a couple of runaway hoes, but they kept getting off the bus at different states. They knew he couldn't do shit for them if he was taking the Greyhound with them. Plus, he had an old crackhead with him. Pimps didn't ride the bus anyway, please! Twan better go on somewhere with his ratchett ass. The hoes knew he was from Louisiana, too. Twan just wondered if his Mama Lela could really do it or if shit would get rough with the top-notch Vegas show call girls competition. That would cause her to start smoking again and leave Twan to scramble for crumbs himself. He didn't know for sure. He needed a kit, which was some strings, a pimp ride, some furs, brims, and jewels. He took another sip of the Henny he had brought on the bus and dozed off.

THE END

Stay tuned, Pimp, for Part II, when Twan hits Vegas! Will he survive and pimp on strong with his Mama Lela or get struck out trying?

About the Author

Hitachi Choparazzi, a.k.a. ChopChop, hails from Arizona by way of New York City and Omaha, Nebraska. His is a typical hood story of growing up in the streets. ChopChop earned his first dollar at eight years old by offering to pump gas for ladies at the local station. That hustle was recognized by the young men who indoctrinated him into street life.

After living in different cities and spending time in the courts and the prison system, Hitachi Choparazzi turned his talents to business, starting a tattoo shop in Phoenix, Arizona. Today, ChopChop is a prolific author who has written thirteen books and has five more projects currently in development. including the Billion Dollar Blueprint Movement, which encourages leadership and entrepreneurship among urban youth.

~ Hitachi Choparazzi ~

Instagram: https://instagram.com/hitachichoparazzi
Facebook: https://facebook.com/hitachi.choparazzi

Pimp of da Ratchetts

Book I of the Pimp of da Ratchetts Series

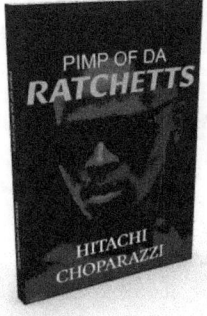

Twan, a recent high school dropout, does what he must to survive in Baton Rouge, Louisiana. Life isn't easy, but he makes it work, even though he's not a d-boy or a gangster. Twan takes a different route. Pimpin' is his game. He doesn't believe there's any such thing as a hoe that's too ratchett. A hoe means dough. Twan doesn't care how ratchett she is or if she's a damned runaway if she pays. For him, all hoes are cash cows.

All Twan wants to do is rep for BR and put the Southside on the map. The only problem is his crackhead mama, Lela, keeps setting him back. His high school sweetheart, Neese, chases him around the BR streets refusing to let him go. And, his new chick threatens to bring the kind of trouble that can get a pimp killed or double digits in the pen. Will Twan get trapped or cracked trying to pimp BR onto the map?

Send the order form with your check or money order to:
Chop-A-Style Publishing, PO Box 693, Chino Hills, CA 91709

Name

Address 1

Address 2

City   State   ZIP

Phone   Email

	Quantity	Quantity x $14.99	U.S. Shipping and Handling - $2.70 each	Total
Pimp of da Ratchetts				

Office Use Only:

Received: _____   Check/MO Date: _____   Check/MO#: _____

Date Mailed: _____   Tracking #: _____

Questions? Call (909) 536-0110 or email orders@chopastylepublishing.com